With You in Spirit

WITH YOU IN SPIRIT

a novel

STEVEN COOPER

alyson books
los angeles

MANUFACTURED IN THE UNITED STATES OF AMERICA.

THIS TRADE PAPERBACK ORIGINAL IS PUBLISHED BY ALYSON PUBLICATIONS,
P.O. BOX 4371, LOS ANGELES, CALIFORNIA 90078-4371.
DISTRIBUTION IN THE UNITED KINGDOM BY TURNAROUND PUBLISHER SERVICES LTD.,
UNIT 3, OLYMPIA TRADING ESTATE, COBURG ROAD, WOOD GREEN,
LONDON N22 6TZ ENGLAND.

FIRST EDITION: AUGUST 2003

03 04 05 06 07 a 10 9 8 7 6 5 4 3 2 1

ISBN 1-55583-783-2

LIBRARY OF CONGRESS CATALOGING-IN-PUBLICATION DATA

COOPER, STEVEN, 1961–

WITH YOU IN SPIRIT : A NOVEL / STEVEN COOPER.—1ST ED.

ISBN 1-55583-783-2

1. MARTHA'S VINEYARD (MASS.)—FICTION. 2. FATHERS—DEATH—FICTION.
3. MOTHERS AND SONS—FICTION. 4. GAY MEN—FICTION. I. TITLE.

PS3603.O68267W58 2003

813'.6—DC21 2003049632

CREDITS

COVER ILLUSTRATION BY JACK GALLAGHER.

COVER DESIGN BY MATT SAMS.

To my parents and my sister, Nancy,
for their unwavering love and support,
and to Jean Stone,
who always knows when my behind needs a kick

Acknowledgments

The following people (in order of appearance) have made everything complete: David O'Leary, Cara London, Deborah Weiner, Pierre Taylor, Linda Roghaar, Angela Brown. Thank you.

One

Certain things are true.

Gay men have good skin because they discover moisturizers very early in life.

If the Bionic Woman were truly bionic, she would have had a bionic vagina and her orgasms would have knocked California off the Richter scale. (This knowledge is something I extract from my precocious childhood and those early, perhaps premature, lessons Mother taught us about reproductive health, always predicated by her insistence that, where women are concerned, orgasm is a right, not a privilege.)

Black is beautiful.

So are children.

Other than that, I cannot say. I have learned not to believe too much else. I work in an accounting office with a pool of women who wear perfume I would never have bought my mother. My mother is an elegant woman with elegant features, cheekbones galore, Bette Davis eyes, just the right hand gestures, and priceless jewelry that dangles from her *Swan Lake* neck. She is the Leona Helmsley of municipal parking, having inherited her family's business, which supplies parking meters to curbsides around the world. She is Palm Beach in the winter, St. Moritz in the spring, the Vineyard in the summer, and wherever she feels like in the fall.

But now she's in jail for murdering my father.

And I know she didn't do it. I believe it's my job to prove it. That's why I'm here. To tell the truth.

Two

My father's body was found floating facedown in the waters off Chappaquiddick. Naturally, everyone eyed the bridge and figured a Kennedy did it.

Not me.

Unlike most in my generation (born 1965, lost virginity at seventeen, experimented with drugs at eighteen, repented at twenty, and moved on) I am not a wholehearted Kennedy-basher. Besides, my father's death (murder?) happened during an election year. The Kennedys were busy.

So was Mother. She was out searching for Father the same ghoulish evening that, according to the medical examiner, he died. He had gone out for a drive or a walk after one of their heated arguments (I'm not sure what the argument was about, and Mother isn't telling); I think Mother had even thrown a bottle of vintage wine at him, which stained my poor father with bloodlike splatter, though he hadn't even been cut, of course, the broken glass landing in jigsaw-puzzle pieces well behind him. He was unhurt but very angry and quite soiled, so he took off in a huff. A mating ritual, I suspect.

Mother, the elegant Celeste Garrison Hoffenstein (affectionately known as Cele to her tony cronies), was seen driving around town in both a rage and a Range Rover, and, unlucky for her, near the water.

The police, of course, discovered the broken bottle of wine while searching, warrant in hand, the Hoffenstein house, known as Sea Valley in certain social circles because of the way it expansively occupies a sloping cleavage between two mounds of sand dune and cliff. (I call it *Entre Tetas,* meaning, in Spanish, "Between Tits.") What the police never did find was the object that smashed my father's skull (the medical examiner had ruled the cause of death as "severe trauma to the head, caused by an object of blunt force"), but they did find blood on my mother's hands, which they refused to believe was her own, caused by her careless and spastic way of clearing the dining room floor of broken glass. She had cut herself, of course, and bled. There was blood on the doorknobs of *Entre Tetas* and blood on the steering wheel of Mother's Range Rover. But would it have made any difference if police had believed her story about the broken glass? I don't think so. Mother and Father shared the same blood type. The blood on her hands might as well have been my father's.

And don't get me started about DNA. Suffice it to say that judges in the Commonwealth of Massachusetts love to hate DNA evidence much the way I love to hate judges across the state (except Judge Romero Pontiac de Corona, with whom I used to sleep until he left me for a twenty-three-year-old trophy boy who rode horses, and apparently judges, rather deftly; there are no hard feelings, of course, when you consider that Romero introduced me to the current love of my life and left me with a very good recipe for paella).

The important thing is this: I believe Cele. I wasn't there, of course. This is all her account. But I believe her. Father had been acting oddly, keeping to himself, mumbling about ghosts and lesbian detective novels, and going off for long business trips to third world countries where municipalities don't worry about parking meters since few people can afford private cars.

"So why waste your time?" I would ask him.

He would simply shake his head and maybe shrug.

My father, Colin Lightfoot Hoffenstein (his mother was a Native American, his father a Jew who fled the Nazis), was a good man. He rarely barked at us children (there are four of us), and the only time he raised his voice to Cele was over business matters, and this never really bothered me; I found it amusing to hear two adults, two accomplished and incredibly civilized and aristocratic adults, scream at each other about parking meters. Colin was solid. A big man with big hands and wide shoulders, a hearty John Wayne face—save for the Indian eyes and quasi-Jewish nose—and a pile of thick white hair that even when he died at sixty-six had not receded. He wasn't fat, just large and imposing, but his voice was soft as a purr. My mother wore the claws in the family. She was the lion. She had to be. The survival of her family and her family business depended on her. Hear her roar.

Too bad the board of directors didn't.

She was the only dissenting vote when the board, two years ago, voted to have me thrown out of the corporation. *My family's* corporation. How dare they? Well, rumors abounded—how, I'll never know—that I'd been bedding down all sorts of municipal officials in order to land lucrative contracts for our company's parking meters. Simply untrue. Of course, if I'd been a female and had landed on the faces of any of those very same board members, I'd have been tenured and given a delightful raise. But no, rumors were fabricated to oust me, the unabashed homosexual (that's *unabashed,* not flagrant or flamboyant), from the company that my own mother nourished like another child at her breast, to rid the board of the dirty image of man and man, dick in anus. My mother screamed, she hollered and shouted; she pummeled the large conference table with her fists and flung her legal pad like a Frisbee across the room. It did no good.

Buh-bye.

And so I picked myself up by my jockstrap and took all the accounting skills I love to hate to the firm of Meyer & Meyer.

Perhaps it was fate, perhaps just a homocosmic joke on the rest of the world that the biggest client I should be assigned to would be King Products, makers of Sensuale Condoms, many of which I've used while gliding up the asshole of my partner, Pedro (the current love of my life), who, incidentally, thinks it ridiculous that I should attempt to find the truth behind the death of my father. Then again, Pedro thinks a lot of things are ridiculous, like cleaning the house, driving with a valid license, and keeping his flatulence to himself. But after six years I figure I love him.

"Gray? Are you coming?"

That's him now. He's not the most patient man in the world, but then again, I'm not the most prompt. We're late for the opera because I've been staring in the mirror wondering whether or not in my mid thirties I'm a strong candidate for Botox. Probably not. But aging in a gay world that adores youth is a hard thing to do.

Pedro is two years younger than me, which he reminds me of quite often. He says he has more energy, a clearer mind, and a harder dick because of his youth. I remind him, in turn, that two years does not constitute a generation gap and that he ought to stop behaving like a hemorrhoid. He's six-one, dark and fit. Not overly muscled, not underly tanned. His eyes are green and he is, indeed, hung like a horse. And I say this with no disrespect to my own horse, Capture (Capture This! at competition, Cap or Cappie when we're alone together, Fucking Asshole when he won't cooperate), who is also hung like a horse.

"Graydove, do you hear me?"

"Yes, I do, Pedro, and don't call me that."

I don't much like when people use my formal name. I love the name, but it suggests my parents were, perhaps, trying pretentiously to be erudite when filling out my birth certificate, when really all they wanted was for at least one of their children to honor, if not represent, a family ancestry.

Graydove comes from my Native American grandmother, and I'm proud of that, but Gray is fine with me. If I were born a girl I was to be named simply Dove. Like the soap—excuse me, *beauty bar.*

"We're going to be late," he whines.

"We already are," I say, and I hear, moments later, Pedro mimicking me in a child's voice down the hallway. *We already are, we already are.*

"What opera are we seeing?" I ask. For the life of me I can't remember. I'm distracted so often now. My mind constantly wanders down the serpentine roads of my imagination, hoping to find Father hitchhiking my way.

"You know," he says, joining me in the hall, patting my behind. "*Carmen.*"

"Not *La Traviata*?"

"What's the difference?"

I look at him in disbelief. "I'm wearing *Italian* cologne," I tell him. "I like my cologne to match the opera."

Pedro laughs and kisses my cheek. His sexy shadow of a beard lightly scratches my face. "You're too much of a fag."

But really I'm not. I'm just enough.

Three

Detective Plotzman won't listen to me. I've come all the way out to the Vineyard to demand a meeting with the police investigators, and they're treating me, the *bereaved,* a surviving family member, like a criminal.

I did not come out here for this.

I did not feign laryngitis and raspily tell my boss I couldn't come into work, drive my car all the way to Falmouth, park it on the ferry, and arrive some three hours after leaving Boston at the crowded docks of Vineyard Haven only to be ignored by some half-brained, small-dicked, pockmarked townie cop. I am the *bereaved.* My father has been dead only a year.

"I will not be ignored," I announce to the detective.

He smiles. "We're not ignoring you, Mr. Hoffenstein. We simply have other things on our agenda. You should have made an appointment."

"No," I correct him, "you should have made an appointment. You should have taken a statement from me before you arrested my mother."

The detective shakes his head. "You were on the mainland. You have no idea what happened the night of your father's death. You have no alibi for your mother."

"This is shoddy police work!" I immediately regret saying this, knowing how suburban housewife it sounds.

"I'm sorry," he says. "The district attorney's office and the state police are in charge of the case now. I suggest you speak to them."

“Fine,” I say, making a dramatic soap opera–like turn for the door.

He stops me.

“Heading to Sea Valley?” he asks.

I sneer. “God, no. It’s November. The house is closed for the season.”

He looks puzzled.

“What is it?” I ask.

“Well, I’m not sure. But I swear I’ve seen lights on in the west wing. And I even think there’s been smoke coming out of the chimney. Maybe one of your siblings is in town.”

“I don’t think so. They hate it here in the off-season. Too damp, too raw.”

“Oh,” he says. “Well, maybe you’d better go give it a check.”

“Maybe,” I say.

“Hey, Gray,” he calls to me again. “What’s that cologne you’re wearing?”

I lean against the door, open it, and before I pass through I turn once again and say, “Nautica.”

☽

I drive away from the tiny police station, not knowing what to do. I have to make the last ferry back to Falmouth, or I’ll be forced to stay the night at a local inn, or maybe even open *Entre Tetas* for the night and crawl up to my old room and pull out blankets from the storage closets. That idea does not appeal to me. But the feeling that something or someone is lurking about my parents’ Chilmark estate has me bothered and unsettled.

I think about the murderer. The real murderer. Whoever it was that obliterated Father. That person is still out there, lurking somewhere in the shadows of justice, maybe even in our kitchen eating from a box of saltines left over by a guest who had become nauseated on the ferry (it happens).

I consider stopping by Carly Simon’s house. I don’t know

Carly. All these years my family has occupied one of the grandest homes on the island and we've never met its resident star. But I figure now is the time. I think the story of Father's death would make a great song.

I turn toward her driveway but then ask myself, "Gray, what the fuck are you doing? You have an intruder at *Entre Tetas* and here you are trying to win a Grammy!"

I'm stunned with shame and spin the wheel faster than a tornado and race for Chilmark.

And when I get there I see that, sure enough, the west wing lights are on, burning Halloween orange in those deep, dark rooms. And the chimney is puffing out, exhaling ghost-like wisps of smoke into the night.

Four

I must say *Entre Tetas* is haunted. We first noticed this back in the summer of 1972 when Juliet, our housekeeper, dropped dead dusting a Fabergé egg that, if truth be told (and this story is about truth, after all), did not need a dusting and had no place atop the toilet tank anyway.

A massive stroke had killed her.

We heard a couple of thuds and looked at one another and said, "What was that? What was that?" Nobody got up. The family, those of us who were home, was gathered for a screening of *Pink Flamingos,* a movie my parents insisted was an art film. I was seven. When I said I wanted to grow up to be a director just like John Waters, they didn't blanch. They simply said, "Parking meters. Your future is in meters." Of course, I gave up the John Waters notion as soon as I saw Divine eat shit. That was no laughing matter; fecal matter, maybe, but nothing to laugh about. It wasn't until my brother got up to get us all a refill of chardonnay and some Rice Krispies treats that we realized something awful had happened.

"I think Juliet is dead," he announced as he returned to the family room.

My mother chortled. "Huh! Pour the wine and sit down," she ordered.

My father snickered. "Now, kids, only one more glass for each of you...and no slurping!"

We loved wine.

"Mother! Father! I'm serious," my brother cried. "I found Juliet lying on the bathroom floor."

"Is she still there?" my mother asked in a dull whisper, her eyes never moving from the screen.

"Yes," my brother replied. "I think she's dead," he repeated.

"Oh, honey," my mother said, flicking her hand toward my father, "go and see to this."

Colin complied.

He returned white-faced. All the color from the Native American side of his family had drained from his skin.

"She's dead," he confirmed. "And we lost a Fabergé egg."

Truly, my family had loved Juliet. She had become a part of our household, almost a part of the family but over time more like a piece of the furnishing; she was just there. Always. Mopping, washing, drying, folding, and, fatefully, dusting. She even helped our cook, Ginkie, with the family's favorite casseroles. Juliet did everything but wipe our asses clean.

She would have, I am sure, had we asked.

I could never tell her age. I was too young; everyone seemed old. As I grew older, so did she; that may be stating the obvious, but her looks never changed. Her gray eyes, her gray hair—the white skunk-like stripe up the middle—often tied up in a bun lest a loose strand should land in our gazpacho or one of Ginkie's casserole creations, which never, ever, called for human hair.

Juliet followed my parents around the world for years.

Ginkie, who loved her liquor, would stay behind to look after us, but we always loved Juliet the most.

Until she started haunting us.

The parapsychologist Cele brought in to clean the house of Juliet's spirit (a notion I find comical to this day: the irony of having to "clean" the house of a woman who was hired to keep it clean to begin with) informed us that Juliet was only doing friendly haunting, and if we didn't mind, she was going by the name Artemis now and would prefer to be called that.

"Sure," we said. "Whatever."

"Just let her be," Dr. Punch told us. "And remember, this is *friendly* haunting." She said "friendly" with an ethereal inflection, not unlike the tone Glinda took with Dorothy Gale on her way to Oz.

Friendly or not, the spilled milk, the slamming doors, the ringing doorbells became somewhat of a nuisance.

"If this is friendly," Father said, "what, pray tell, is unfriendly?"

"You could wake up with a broomstick up your ass," Dr. Punch replied, smiling like a fairy godmother to us all.

When Dr. Punch was gone, her credentials still a subject of much debate among the Hoffenstein clan, we tried talking to Juliet, er, Artemis, herself.

Mother had a sudden revelation. We saw lightning bolts flash in her eyes. Uh-oh.

"Maybe she feels bad about the egg," Cele announced.

"The egg?" Kirkland asked.

"Well, I'll be damned!" Father bellowed. "Your mother's right," he said, turning to his wife. "Cele, you're a genius." These kinds of comments made for much harmony in our household and, without question, kept Father on the payroll. "Juliet feels bad about the Fabergé egg. We need to convince her it's okay. No great loss."

Mother cleared her throat.

"Play along, dear," Father said affectionately.

"Yes," I said, too innocent, too naive to know better. "If she sees we don't really care about the egg, well, maybe she'll feel free to move on. You know, the guilt might be what's keeping her from crossing over to the other side."

Mother offered me a bemused glance; I remember her looking like the great British actress Maggie Smith. "How does a seven-year-old know anything about 'crossing over to the other side'?"

I smiled. "I've been reading a lot of books about dying."

"Have you?" she asked, still bemused.

"Yes, Mother. Ever since Juliet died I've been very curious about what happens after death."

Cele shook her head. "Nothing happens after death, my dear. You just die. You get stuck in a box and it's over. Eternal blackness. Eternal nothing. Colin, pour me some more sherry."

Father complied. "Well, I think Graydove has a point. In fact, I'm quite sure he has this whole thing figured out."

My younger brother sneered at me. My older sister patted my head.

"Yes, I think we need to rid Juliet of this insane guilt," he continued. "What do you suggest, my wise young son?"

And that's how we came to smash every Fabergé egg in the house. It seemed like a weird twist on the Easter egg hunt. The four children were sent off to all corners of the estate to gather up as many eggs as possible. Once they were collected, we returned to the family room, and from there Father led us out to the shuffleboard court, where we in gay abandon used the eggs as disks and shuffled until we had smashed them all to smithereens. I'd never seen my mother weep until that evening on the east lawn of the house, watching her children destroy the very essence of her glamour. At least that's how she described the experience when, years later, she emerged from Dr. Leventhal's (counseling, hypnosis, aromatherapy) office a recovered woman and a dedicated collector of Limoges boxes.

"Hands off," she warned us.

Our hands were off, but meanwhile, Juliet was off to the other side, having departed this world shortly after the Fabergé egg hunt.

It worked.

Darn it, it worked!

But now, years later, as I sit here at the end of the driveway staring at a home obviously invaded by an intruder, feeling the raw chill of island winter stir around my neck, I assume Juliet is back.

Five

The long driveway ends in a big circle that loops around a majestic elm. I stop the car in the circle and then think better of it and drive through the archway at the end of the house and around to the back. Where there now stands this elegant archway, there used to be a simple two-car garage. My parents never intended for the driveway to sweep around to the back of the property. That is, until Aunt Sadie (Mother's older sister) came over to demonstrate how the blind (which legally she was) could learn to drive (which obviously she hadn't). She was on a crusade—there were even articles written about her in several New England newspapers—to prove that the blind could drive, insisting they could rely on their other senses to maneuver their way. Well, Mother relented and said, "Sure, Sadie, if you really believe in this, we'll give it a whirl."

"After all," my father added, "with the world's blind population licensed to drive, there's certain to be a need for more parking meters."

Sadly, however, the experiment lasted only moments. After successfully coasting down the long Vineyard driveway, Aunt Sadie drove right through the garage door and right through the garage. She came out the other side and landed halfway down the back lawn, where the *tetas* meet the sea.

Mother shook her head. "This isn't going to work," she whispered.

"Oh, I don't know," Father mused. "You can really see the water now from the front of the house."

And, thus, the garage became an archway.

Aunt Sadie broke her wrists and collarbone, but *Entre Tetas* had a new look.

And it was splendid.

I park.

I jiggle my key chain until I find the key I need. I am a little bit, hmm, scared? A little bit excited, perhaps.

I choose the back door by the kitchen. It whines as it opens. I'm standing in a mini foyer of stone and glass. The kitchen smells clean as if, as if, no...Juliet has been cleaning? But it's not freshly clean, I realize. It smells of being vacant and unused, sterile maybe. An old calendar hangs on the refrigerator door. Things like "Colin's birthday," "Leave for Paris," and "Rectal exam" are scribbled among its many days and dates. Mother doesn't throw calendars away. She saves them like photoless photo albums, family pictures without the pictures, appointment-book memoirs.

Too bad this isn't a current calendar. If it were, I could flip back to September 5 and find that Cele had scribbled "Trial begins" in the otherwise empty box.

Her trial lasted two and a half weeks. It was a travesty, a kangaroo court, a spectacle for the press, a three-ring circus, but on the upside it was also the first time I'd seen my whole family in a very long time. Everyone was there. Aunts, uncles, cousins, in-laws, family from both sides. They let Mother do lunch with us during the trial (she never once even mentioned taking off), and we had some sumptuous meals. Sadie still wanted to drive, but we avoided the subject by hiring a stretch limousine to take Mother's entourage to and from our delightful luncheons. The trial was hard on us, especially since all the evidence was circumstantial. In Massachusetts you can convict on circumstantial evidence, and that's what the jury did. I had a hard time believing the jury could sympathize at all with

Mother—she being the very personification of society and elegance; they being the motley crew chosen for, of all things, their ignorance of the crime. The judicial system thinks this is a good thing. ("Have you ever read anything in the newspaper or seen anything on television news about the murder of Colin Hoffenstein?" "No, nothing." "Fine, then, stick around.") I should mention that my father's murder was splashed all over the front pages of newspapers and described in morbid detail by the bob-bing-head anchorpeople of television news. And because my parents lived in so many places in the course of a year, the story made, for a short but vivid time, national head-lines. Thus, someone who knew nothing about Father's murder had either never read a newspaper or never tuned into anything more informative than *Wheel of Fortune*. I find it very hard to believe that Mother was judged by a jury of her peers. Never one to be a snob or look down her Dr. Rhinoplasty nose at anyone for anything (after all, her fortune was in parking meters, not hotels or banking or designer hosiery, and she knew it), Cele admitted to me shortly after the guilty verdict that she felt she had, indeed, been convicted by a trailer park.

I shuffle through the kitchen and push my way into a small dining nook and then to the formal dining room, very dark and still and velvet. I can smell the sea in here and the way the salt lingers in the wood of the house, and for a moment tears come to my eyes; I'm brought back so poignantly to my child-hood of ocean swims and chattering teeth and late-afternoon storms with brilliant cracking lightning.

I hear music now. And my skin turns goosey. My hair stands on end and a chill goes the length of my body. It is clas-sical music. Strauss, I think. Juliet's favorite. She would play Strauss, occasionally Mozart and Bach, while she cleaned. I am convinced. Juliet is here. Now. She's back. It is a strain for me to call her Artemis. But I do.

"Artemis? It's me, Graydove..."

No answer.

"Artemis? It's okay. You can reveal yourself."

Still no answer.

I move into the front foyer and can barely make out the orange light burning far off in the west wing living room. I don't want to get any closer.

The music is louder, though; it's definitely coming from that side of the house.

"Juliet? Perhaps you call yourself Juliet again? Please, let's talk."

Suddenly I understand.

She is back. Upset by my mother's conviction, she has come back from the other side to keep things in order while Mother is in jail. This is so in character for Juliet; it's just something she would do. She was always such a sensitive woman, always a parental figure, always the fixer of broken hearts, souls, psyches.

"Juliet," I say, nearly singing, "you didn't have to come back for us. We're okay. Really."

I now with confident steps breeze through the house to the room where orange lights are burning. I'm eager as I step across the threshold, the sounds of Strauss filling the air like the sudden wallop and whoosh of gulls soaring from cliff to sea. I'm in the room.

It feels like everything is on fire.

My skin is hot.

My eyes water.

There, sitting in a rocking chair, facing away from me, is a shadowy figure with long wispy hair, her hands in her lap, rocking ever so slowly to the rhythm of the music.

It must be her. "Juliet!" I cry. "Juliet!"

The chair stops rocking. The woman gets up abruptly. Spins around.

"You asshole," she says. "It's me."

I can see her face now.

"Juliet is still very dead," I'm told.

Yes, I nod my head, stepping forward to hug and kiss my sister, Chaka.

Six

Glib. That's what Chaka calls me.

"You're so glib," she always says.

"And you're so *not* African-American," I always retort.

She hates the truth. She hates having the mirror held up to her 40-year-old white face. All these years, and she's still a Caucasian. She's tried Afro-Sheen, Jheri Curl, and a lot of tanning, but my sister, who once confided in me that she had always wished she were Coretta Scott King (a bereft black woman is beautiful, holy, and righteous, she explained) could never quite convince anyone that her roots belonged to any other tribe than, maybe, the Navajo, or perhaps the lost tribe of Israel. "Lost" might best describe Chaka (real name: Norma Lee), who has tried so hard to seek an identity that she has never quite found herself. At forty, she insists she's an artist, but she's hardly starving, as she draws a hefty allowance from Parking Meters of the World, and I've yet to see a finished painting or sculpture, save for a charcoal drawing of Cicely Tyson that she refers to as "Self-Portrait."

"I was raised glib," I always argue.

"Don't blame all your shortcomings on your childhood," she will argue back.

"Who says glib is a shortcoming?"

Now, happening upon each other at *Entre Tetas,* we embrace.

"What are you doing here?" I ask her.

"Same as you."

"Looking for Juliet?"

"Juliet is dead, Gray. When are you going to accept that?"

"I accept it."

We stand apart from each other and smile. We love and we hate each other. We are the closest of the four siblings. She's the firstborn; I came four years later. Skye, now twenty-five, is winding down a semisuccessful career as a fashion model (Kmart, Wal-Mart, Petsmart), and trying to hone her skills as a musician (guitar, piano, triangle) by putting the poetry of Sylvia Plath to song (depressing). And then there's Kirkland. Oh, Lord Kirkland. How we worship you. He's thirty and has eschewed the family business for his own personal and self-impressed fortune in Silicon Valley. All the members of his sales team drive Porsches (a requirement) and have big dicks (the women too). He sets the pace by driving a Ferrari and wearing a permanent sneer as if he just cannot stand anyone who earns less than a million dollars annually (*one mill,* he would say). Kirk-the-jerk. We have a hate-hate relationship. I hate him; he hates me. My mother loves him, because, well, he was the first child to post a net worth as great as that of her and my father. She does not love him *more.* She just loves him *special,* she says.

I'm not bitter.

"Have you eaten?" I ask my sister.

"Yes, on the ferry."

"You took the ferry over?"

"No, I swam."

"No need to be like that," I tell her. "I came in on the noon crossing."

"Me too," she says.

"How odd we didn't see each other."

"So?"

"So, what?"

We're standing in this lit but darkened chamber, looking like shadows rather than people. The music continues.

"So what have you found out?" my sister asks.

"Nothing. Nothing at all."

"Me neither."

"Been to visit Mother?"

"She looks awful."

"I didn't very well think she'd blossom in prison."

"I'm almost ready to give up," my sister says.

"What? How can you say that?"

She shakes her head and waves her hands as if, by pushing the air around, the mystery surrounding my father's death will somehow disperse. "It's been over a year, Gray. We've started this little quest of ours too late, I'm afraid."

"Too late?"

She laughs, not a funny ha-ha laugh but rather a tiny self-inflicted chuckle of disgust. "Mother's been convicted. She's in jail. Case closed."

I can't believe what I'm hearing. "I can't believe what I'm hearing," I tell her.

"It took a year for the case to go to trial," she argues. "Nothing came to light then. I sincerely doubt we'll get anywhere now."

I shut off the music. I put my face in hers. "I do not want to hear you talk like that, Chaka Khan Hoffenstein. I won't have you giving up."

"I'm sorry," she says, and begins to weep. She flips her dreadlocks out of the way and wipes her eyes.

This is a rare moment. For us. My sister is vulnerable here in this room of echoes and dark furniture (custom-made, shipped in by private ferry). She is usually on the offense.

I sit her down. I am right beside her. I put my hand on her shoulder and lean my head against hers. "You didn't come here to give up, did you?"

"Huh?"

"You didn't take the boat over just to get here and quit."

She sniffles. "No. I suppose not."

"You don't believe Mother killed Father, do you?"

She plops my head aside and bolts up in front of me. Her eyes are whole seas of torment. "God, no!" she cries. "How can you say that?"

"Then why, Chaka, why are you here?"

She says nothing. She turns away from me; I talk to her back—I'm reminded of any number of those scenes in daytime dramas, the way characters are forced to emote, to demand, to talk to a shoulder blade.

"If you must know," she begins.

"I must."

The silence drags on.

Finally, she faces me. "I came here to see Brenda Cloudholder."

"Brenda Cloudholder? The Voodoo Lady in Oak Bluffs?"

My sister sits again. She smiles. Genuinely. "She does not do voodoo, Gray."

"But Dad used to always call her the Voodoo Lady."

"Yes, I know. But she isn't into voodoo. She never has been. She's a medium."

"She looks like a large to me."

"This would not be a good time to be an asshole."

"Well, why the hell did you come here to see Brenda?"

Chaka hesitates. She stammers, she stutters, she looks away, and I sense her shoulder blade is not far behind.

But I am wrong.

"I want to do a séance," she blurts out.

"A what?"

"A séance. Tonight."

Seven

A steady rain splatters the windows. An island storm, typical for the Vineyard. I open the front door of *Entre Tetas* and take a huge whiff of the damp air. The night is purple and wet, and puddles in the driveway flinch with every drop of rain.

She arrives in a low-riding Yugo that belches and knocks and betrays any other sound a muffler might muffle. *How is it that the Steamship Authority actually let this thing on the boat?* I wonder. My wonder is interrupted, however, by the spastic creak of car doors opening and by the presence of a man I assume is not Brenda Cloudholder.

"Derderva," he says.

"Say what?"

"My name is Derderva."

And you didn't kill your parents? I want to ask, but I don't dare say such a thing to this man, not with that distant Jeffrey Dahmer look in his eyes. He is tall, pencil-thin, with dark eyes. He is wearing mascara, I think. His skin is whiter than chalk. He smells vaguely of cheese, maybe death. Maybe the death of cheese.

"I am Ms. Cloudholder's chauffeur."

I don't recognize his cologne. "You drive her around in a Yugo?"

"It was bequeathed to her. She drives it for someone from the other side."

"Of town?" I ask. "Oak Bluffs?"

He smiles a thin smile and shakes his head. "No, my dear," he says. "The *other* side."

There used to be a gay bar in Boston called the Other Side. But that was before my time. It was even before my puberty. Derderva, I'm sure, would not know a gay bar from a Hershey bar (yes, there's a twisted double entendre there somewhere), so I resist the reference and urge him and his employer to come in out of the rain.

Brenda emerges from the Yugo.

She is huge.

I realize, suddenly, that the car is not a low-rider after all.

Brenda is dressed in a black silky thing with lacy sleeves and a lacy neckline. She is wearing dark sunglasses and carrying a cat.

"Meow."

"This is Lourdes," Brenda says, extending her pet's paw, "and I'm Brenda. Brenda Cloudholder."

"I'm Graydove Hoffenstein. And I'm allergic," I tell her, forsaking the paw.

"I am so sorry, my child," Brenda says, "but I can't go anywhere without Lourdes."

Derderva steps forward and pats the feline's neck, then does the same thing to his boss. *The same thing!* "Lourdes is a seeing-eye cat," he says soberly.

I am not *even* going to ask.

"And she must accompany Brenda," he adds sternly, "or there will be no séance."

I smile an innocent smile, feigning genuine concern but feeling suspicious that this must be what it's like when, instead of visiting a carnival, the carnival comes to visit you. "Well, I have a lovely idea," I tell them. "Why, Derderva, don't you be Brenda's guide for the evening and leave Lourdes in the car? She'd probably appreciate the night off."

A clap of thunder. A strike of lightning. Brenda raises her free hand to the air. The drama of nature goes quiet.

"Never mind," I say.

"Derderva, come back for me in two hours."

He pecks her cheek.

"You could have joined us. You could have been her seeing-eye chauffeur," I call to him as he retreats to the Yugo.

☽

Inside, I introduce Chaka to Brenda and Lourdes.

"A seeing-eye cat?" Chaka asks.

"Yes," I reply. "This is something new to you?"

"Well, no," Chaka assures me with lying eyes. "I just can't see how the cat can guide Ms. Cloudholder while resting in her arms."

"I've had her trained," the enormous lady replies. She is not an obese woman. Yes, she is rotund, and there is enough fat on her to defy liposuction, but her enormity is more in her structure, in the architecture of her facade. She has a big face, a wide forehead, a neck as thick as a tree trunk. Her breasts rival airbags (inflated); her cleavage is daunting. But she has very small hands. As she describes the training of Lourdes I can't help fixating on her dainty little hands, her delicate fingers. Chaka is listening intently. "She is not a seeing-eye pet in the traditional sense," Brenda concedes. "I never put her down, but she guides me so well. Two meows mean go to the left. One meow means go to the right."

"Uh-huh," I utter.

"Three long meows mean I'm at the top or bottom of the stairs," she continues, "and three short, quick meows mean I'm about to be hit by a truck."

I roll my eyes publicly, here, because Brenda Cloudholder cannot see out of hers. Even Chaka looks doubtful. But she simply shrugs and shakes her head.

"What are you getting us into?" I ask her.

"Shh!" she begs me. "The woman is *blind,* not *deaf.*"

We move into the formal living room; Lourdes meows the lefts and rights accordingly. Suddenly I discern three short, quick meows and I instantly look for a barreling eighteen-wheeler, but then I realize, of course, it is only Brenda purring back to her pet.

We sit.

At a round table, of course. It is, so it happens, a table with some mystical history of its own. My Aunt Sadie insists she had a near-death experience playing Hearts with some of her favorite cronies at this very same table, many years ago when my parents first opened the Vineyard compound. Suddenly the game stopped, she says, and she saw this beautiful white light and she felt herself drifting toward it; she heard voices, saw faces of those who had already died; the dead relatives told her what cards the others were holding and she realized it was not her time to die. Instead she went back and won the game. But I think somehow she got caught cheating that night and made up the story to cover her ass. You'd think it would be impossible for a blind woman to cheat at Hearts, but now, sitting here with blind Brenda, I'm not so sure.

The lights are low.

I can still hear the rain.

We hold hands.

Brenda whispers something.

"I'm sorry?"

"You weren't meant to hear that," she tells me.

Lourdes farts.

"You weren't meant to hear that either," Brenda says.

Her voice is low, with subtle vibrato and a smoky rasp. In many ways she sounds like a cave exhaling into the night.

"You are searching for your father," she thunders.

"Yes," Chaka says, way too seriously in my opinion.

"His name is Colin Lightfoot Hoffenstein," Brenda chants.

"Yes," Chaka replies.

"He was killed just over a year ago?"

"Yes."

"His body was found in water."

"Yes."

"I am seeing a rock."

And I am seeing someone who obviously read the Braille edition of *The Boston Globe.* Nothing Brenda is telling us is new, unusual, psychic, or surprising.

Lourdes farts again.

"He died a violent death," Brenda continues.

"Funny," I say, "I can't for the life of me think of a recent murder that wasn't."

Brenda fans the latest cat fart in my face and smiles.

"Why would someone want to kill him?" Chaka asks.

Brenda suddenly claps her hands. "Maybe he'll tell us."

There is silence. All but the purring of the cat, the hollow sounds of the wind and the rain outside. A toilet upstairs is running. Someone needs to jiggle the handle.

I look at Chaka. She responds with a terse, admonishing stare. Like maybe I'm not taking this séance seriously enough. Puhl-e-e-eze, I beg her with loaded eyes, the only thing *medium* about this woman is the milkshake she has for breakfast.

"Your father is here. In this room!" Brenda cries. "Can you feel him? Can you?"

Chaka lowers her head and begins to weep softly. "Yes," she whispers. "Father, talk to us."

I look up, hear nothing, see nothing, feel nothing. "So, Dad," I say, "seen Elvis?"

Chaka elbows me in the side. But what, I wonder, explains the whack upside my head? Wasn't Chaka. Wasn't Brenda (she can't see my head). And it wasn't a paw.

Oh, my.

Oy vey! my Jewish half wants to scream.

"Can we hear him?" Chaka asks. "Can we hear his voice?"

"He will talk through me," Brenda tells us.

"Well, fine, then," I say. "Dad, let's cut to the chase. Who killed you?"

No answer.

"Really, Father. Surely you know Mother is in jail for this. Chaka and I are determined to get her out. You're our last hope, Dad. Come through for us."

No reply.

"Dad? Do you really want your darling Cele sitting in jail for the rest of her life? That doesn't seem fair. If you love her let her go. Set her free!"

Still, nothing.

"Maybe he wants her to stay in jail," I tell the others. "You know, this way she won't give herself to another man."

This time the whack upside the head knocks me out of my chair.

"Gray!" Chaka cries.

"I'm okay," I assure her.

"Father, you were never this physical with us when you were alive. Do you disapprove of this séance?"

The lights in the room go out. The table starts to vibrate. My hand tightens around my sister's. She is scared. I am scared. The storm outside roars.

Lourdes jumps onto the table. Her claws *tick-tick-tick* across the surface like feline tap shoes.

A mournful sound fills the room. A moan, a groan. A window breaks.

Brenda Cloudholder rises from the table. A light from outside funnels into the room and casts a moonlike glow on her face. She lifts her hands to the air, and like a great diva she begins to sing:

At first I was afraid, I was petrified...
Thinking I could never live without you as my bride,

But then I spent so many nights thinking how you did me wrong.
I grew strong.
I learned how to wear a thong.
And so you're back, from outer space...

The great anthem continues, and I am both moved and deeply disturbed.

Lourdes licks my face. Her tongue tastes like a last-call martini against my lips.

Eight

Gloria Gaynor killed my father?

She's had a hard enough time making a comeback. You'd think she'd realize that murder is not something that's going to bring back the fans.

"You're taking this all too literally," my sister tells me the following morning as I am throwing my things together for a noon ferry back to Falmouth. "The song was a hint, Gray, not an answer."

"A hint?"

"Sure. Father was trying to send us a message."

"Why doesn't he just come out with it and tell us? What is this message thing? That's not like him. He was always very direct when he was alive."

"So you think."

"What's that supposed to mean?"

"It means we can't assume we knew Father as well as we think we did."

I shake my head. "I believe this Brenda Cloudholder has put a spell on you."

"She doesn't do spells," Chaka says. "She's a medium. Not a witch. And people come from all over the world to seek her help."

"If she's so successful, what explains the Yugo?"

Chaka sits on the bed beside my small knapsack. "It's not the money, Gray. She does this because she has the power. Because she knows she was put here to use it."

"How much did you pay her for last night?"
"Four thousand dollars."
"What? Are you crazy? Four thousand dollars for a performance of 'I Will Survive'? And not a very good one at that?"
"She's closer to Father than you and I have managed to get."
"So you think," I say, giving her a taste of her own remark.
"I want to do another séance," Chaka tells me. She isn't looking at me now. Instead she stares across the room, studying a painting on the wall called *Portrait of a Circumcision,* and waits for a reply. I follow her gaze and wonder what the hell Cele was thinking when she hung this "art" in my bedroom. Had she wanted me to meet my inner child by taking me back to my earliest experience with pain? Had she wanted me to remember and respect my Jewish heritage? The painting showed up one day when I was twelve, just a short time before my bar mitzvah (Native American style; don't ask). Cele said it was an early gift. She had found it in some eclectic artist's colony in the north of Israel. She had paid extra to have the artist sign it (nothing is too good for my Graydove), and he did; his name was Yehuda Picasso, and he claimed to be the illegitimate son of Pablo, the famous artist, and Golda Meir, the former prime minister of Israel. Of course they're both dead now, so it's hard to verify his account, but, heck, the kid's got talent, albeit complicated by his fascination with foreskin.
"No," I say.
Chaka turns to me, having consumed as much of the bris-on-canvas as she cared to. "No?"
"No more séances."
"But Graydove, we've only just begun."
"Begun what? A path down spiritual quackery? Look, Chaka, you want to be black, be black. No one's stopping you. Go crazy. Wear your funky clothes, sing your funky

songs, join the NAACP for all I care, but please, enough of this nonsense about talking to Father."

"The séance has nothing to do with me being black," she says dismissively.

"Maybe not. But, speaking strictly on odds, you have a better chance of being black than we have of talking to Father. And I'm willing to humor you, Queen Latifah, to an extent."

She follows me to the front door.

"I'm staying here for a few more days," she tells me.

"It's not like you have to get back to work."

"Don't begrudge me."

"I don't. But you know, Chaka, maybe if you did hold down a full-time job you wouldn't have so much time on your hands to dream up these bizarre ideas."

The phone rings.

"Go answer it," I tell her. "I gotta run."

"No, wait," she insists. "We're not through."

She backs away into the front sitting room. I hear her pick up the phone. She doesn't say anything, and my curiosity mounts with each silent second. Finally she returns.

"Who was it?"

"I dunno. Nobody was on the other end."

"Well, you were on long enough. Didn't you recognize the voice?"

"Not really," she replies with a puff of disgust. "There was no one there. Just music playing. I didn't recognize the song. But I'm sure it was Streisand."

I roll my eyes, lean forward, kiss her cheek, and I'm gone.

☽

Pedro has surprising news. I'm not thrilled about it, but it appears there's nothing I can do. He's going away.

"My family needs me," he told me when we sat down for dinner the night I returned from the Vineyard.

"Are you mad that I took off without telling you?" I asked him. "Is that what this is all about?"

He snapped his tongue against the roof of his mouth and made a *tsk* sound. He curled his lip and snarled. "No, Gray, baby, this has nothing to do with you. I know you weren't fucking anyone on the Vineyard. Nobody worth fucking stays there in the off-season. My family needs me in Puerto Rico right now. I gotta go, man. They don't ask much from me, so when they do I feel this obligation."

He held his stomach when he said "obligation," indicating that either the sense of obligation was something he felt deep in his gut or that the word was making him ill. I couldn't tell. And I didn't ask. But I did want more details. "What's going on down there?"

"A family emergency," he replied.

I looked across the table until his eyes met mine. They were so deep and brown within their white frames. Masterpieces, really. Portraits of desire. His hair was curly, black and curly and wet-looking, and I remembered that his hair was certainly the first thing that made my heart pound when we first met, because it suggested all the darkness and mystery of his nest of pubic hair and the sexy, Latin way his penis might lie there like a snake in the jungle. His skin was so smooth, so soft, so brown. His smile gleamed. His lips were full and had edges that drove me wild when they came close to pry open my own. And now I wanted to rip his clothes off right there at the dining room table, lick every muscle of his body and watch him shoot his milky stuff, but I sensed an absence on his part. As if he had already boarded the plane and left.

He wouldn't tell me what the family emergency was. I said that was unfair and unacceptable. After all, he had been my partner for six years; we told each other everything, did we not? Hadn't I told him about the séance? Well, no. Not yet.

I kiss him goodbye at the airport. His tongue enters my

mouth, and it's hot as it makes the rounds of my throat. We kiss passionately like that for what seems like hours, pressing close to each other, sharing the hardness of our erections, acknowledging with this special closeness that we are who we are and we are who we've been: lovers, partners, boyfriends, husbands, man and man.

"Excuse me, gentlemen, I'm going to have to ask you to step aside unless your row's been called."

So says Candy the flight attendant, standing at the entrance to the Jetway, taking tickets, smiling her GED smile. Our kiss is apparently blocking the boarding of other passengers.

Pedro pulls away. He removes his airline ticket from the inside pocket of his cotton blazer. He gives me one last kiss, sans tongue, and steps forward to board.

"I love you," I tell him.

"I'll love you forever," he says to me with a rhythm in his voice, a cadence I have never heard before.

❩

I'm alone in my apartment missing Pedro when a thought jolts me like a sudden case of diarrhea. My brain gets cramped. My mind starts to race. Soon my imagination is spouting all sorts of ugly, messy conclusions.

I remember that Chaka's ex-husband, Billy Bose, a white man who drove an El Camino (she left him for a black man who drives a BMW), once threatened to shoot Father fifty times in the head.

Nine

The confrontation happened years ago at the Ritz-Carlton in Boston.

Father and Bobby Bose were arguing over tea in China.

My parents had offered Bobby a job, and he had insulted them by saying he wouldn't work for their parking meter empire "for all the tea in China"; Father responded by saying that it was too bad Billy preferred living like white trash out of an El Camino (how else does one live out of such a "car"? I ask) to putting in an honest day's work, and he argued that the amount of tea in China, truth be told, was grossly overestimated; the biting remarks about the El Camino went over Bobby's head, but Father's comment about the tea sure got Bobby Bose mighty upset, and he insisted he knew more about the Far East than anybody in the hotel suite, if not the entire hotel, because he had served in Vietnam (which, of course, would later provide an explanation for both his knowledge of Chinese tea and his personality disorder). A fight ensued. The two men had bursting red faces, loud bellicose voices, and veins popping from their necks. Their saliva became projectile; they started to push and shove. Mother ushered Kirkland and Skye from the suite. Chaka (then, Norma) and I were allowed to stay and watch. I tried to wallop Bobby over the head with an antique lamp, but Norma grabbed it from my hands and warned me not to take sides.

Mother dialed room service.

The men stopped the battle when, a short time later, a waiter wheeled in a cart of cups and saucers and plates of biscuits and announced, "Afternoon tea, as you ordered."

"Tea?" Father asked.

"Tea!" Bobby Bose roared.

"Peace," my mother said gently. "Let's have peace."

"Peace, my ass," Bobby told everyone. (At first I thought I heard "piece of my ass," to which I almost replied "I'd rather be gunned down by a Vietnamese firing squad.") "There will be no peace in this lifetime!" he cried. "No peace! Only war. I know, I've been there. And we didn't have afternoon tea."

He collapsed onto the foldout sofa and cried heavily. My sister tried to comfort him, but in his embarrassment he pushed her away, rose from the sofa, and made for the door. "Mr. Hoffenstein, you so much as suggest I come to work for you ever again," Bobby said, his eyes calm, his voice even, "and I'll put fifty bullets in your head."

Then he left and we had tea. The scones were very good.

Why I suddenly remember this now, I can't understand. Surely it was a major moment in the history of our family. Surely we took pictures that day, put them in the family album with the description "Day Bobby Threatened to Kill Daddy" beneath each one.

I suppose no one ever thought he was serious. About the threat, I mean. And he had been out of the picture for years by the time Father was killed. Chaka and Bobby were divorced long ago, and their marriage was a moment of Hoffenstein history we'd all rather rewrite. Sure, his last words to us were "I'll get revenge. I'll make this whole family suffer," but apparently Bobby had failed to realize we could suffer no more than we already had the four years he and Norma were together. Imagine the heartbreak of seeing your sister wed a man in a JCPenney leisure suit. A man with giant hands and a serious overbite. A man who had nicknamed the Venus de Milo "Stumpgirl."

In the year since my father's death I have gone up and down his list of friends and found not an enemy among them. I thought I had reviewed everyone who could possibly have had a motive. Perhaps you think that a fruitless exercise, but in Mother and Father's social circle some of your best friends are your worst enemies. Still, no suspects there.

This much I know: No one at the company killed Father. I have investigated every single executive who may have wanted to remove Father in order to get closer to Mother. I have also investigated every single board member who may have conspired to do away with Father to break the family's hold on the company (as it is, with Father gone the company was able to do away with its troublesome homo), but the executives and the board members all had perfect alibis and crocodile sympathy at the time of Father's death. I hired a private investigator to look into Father's extramarital activities on his plentiful journeys abroad. The investigator, a man who actually looked at home in a JCPenney leisure suit, reported back with a sad face and a sunken posture. Seems that Colin Lightfoot Hoffenstein had no extramarital activities overseas to speak of. And when he was home, Father was *home,* under the somewhat domineering watch of my somewhat domineering mother, without a moment to so much as swim a lap in our indoor pool undisturbed by Cele's incessant blowing of the whistle that hung from her necklace of diamonds, rubies, and sapphires.

The whistle was sterling.

My mother was not and is not Leona Helmsley. She merely ran a tight ship. She could laugh at her own controlling self; she could joke about her fanatic obsessions. Most important, the woman could compromise. And that is what saved her from being hated.

If Father disobeyed her, she would simply put on a heinous-smelling cologne, eat pickles in bed, and wet the sheets. She had many recipes for torture. Some made Father vomit. Others made him laugh. And always, after the torture was afflicted and endured, they would talk out the problem and would compromise. He would go to Europe for five days (not for two weeks as he had planned, and not for two days as she had first insisted); he would buy twelve new suits (not twenty as he had wanted, and not four as she had demanded). They would vacation in Mustique (not Sea World as he had wished, and not Madagascar as she had planned). They were very different, but they were very compatible. They loved each other deeply. Yes, Mother had the capacity to throw a bottle of wine at his head—as she did the night of his murder—but she did not have the heart, the means, the motive, the need to kill him.

I had Kirkland investigated too. After all, the only interest he has ever shown in the family has been monetary. It was fair to suspect he might want Father to disappear, to bring him that much closer to Mother's money, if not the entire will. Kirkland checked out. I was disappointed, but he checked out. Seems he was spotted frolicking with his secretary's daughter on a pink-velvet beach in Bermuda at the time of Father's death. The leisure-suited investigator produced a fuzzy, albeit believable, photograph of Kirkland (a my-shit-doesn't-stink smile on his face, a young girl's breast in his hand) that could have sold handsomely to any number of tabloids had anyone really cared much about the life of Kirkland Elizabeth (he was conceived during one of Mother and Father's many crossings aboard the *QEII*) Hoffenstein. Needless to say, no one did, which is probably of enormous benefit to Kirkland Elizabeth because my investigator also determined, through wise and intrepid research, that Young Girl With Breast was no more than sixteen years old.

Friends, neighbors, household help didn't kill him either. I had them all checked out too. Especially Ina and Morty Russelbaum, who used to visit *Entre Tetas* regularly; I always caught them snooping in wings of the house normally off-limits to guests. To this day I have no idea what they were looking for, but their behavior made them very suspicious to me. Detective Plotzman didn't like them too much either. After all, his first encounter with the Russelbaums was met with this statement: "What's a nice Jewish boy like you doing in a cop uniform? Jews aren't cops! And Jews definitely don't live on the Vineyard *year round*!" He was horrified. I was horrified. I know for sure Ina Russelbaum took things from the house, because one time I planted an ounce of Mother's foul-smelling perfume (Eau de Torture) in an empty bottle of an otherwise very expensive perfume (Eau de Prenup, or something like that), and sure enough, on a subsequent visit three weeks later, Ina showed up stinking like a Miami landfill on a hot August day.

Ina and Morty had alibis too. They were both undergoing liposuction at the time of the murder. It was a two-for-one deal at a Palm Springs spa. Ina later complained that the spa director took one look at her and said, "Honey, you are the two for one."

I guess it took seeing Mother escorted in handcuffs from that austere and silent courtroom to trigger the innermost parts of my memory. I guess it took seeing the Queen of Parking Meters behind bars, stripped of her purpose in life, of her darling way of kissing the world good morning, of her love affair with being a lady, relegated to a cell not at all her color, for me to reach a clarity heretofore unreachable.

I call Chaka.

"You're crazy!"

"No, I'm not. Think about it. Bobby was nuts. And probably capable of murder. I mean, he *threatened* Dad. Let's make a list of all the people who threatened Father's life..."

"What?"

"C'mon, let's do it... Let's see, there was Bobby, and...and...hmm, who else out there threatened to kill Father?"

"I see your point, Gray. But I can't believe you think Bobby would ever make good on his threat. He's not that smart."

"True. Very true," I said. "But he hated us even more because of the divorce. Hate is a tremendous motivator."

"But we were divorced ten years ago. I don't even know where Bobby is these days."

"Good point. We have to find him."

I hear a sigh come toward me through the phone line. "Well, I can't do anything right now," my sister tells me. "I have a meeting tonight."

"A meeting?"

"Urban League."

Click.

Chaka divorced Bobby Bose because Bobby Bose was stupid. That was the party line. You know, that's what we told gossip columnists and other alleged journalists who needed to know the dirt on society's Breakup of the Week.

But secretly I knew Chaka had broken up with Bobby Bose because he was not only stupid, he was also not black enough. Of course he wasn't black enough. He was white. Chaka had just about abandoned everything white in her life, and the only thing left to go was Bobby. I suspect she had already begun her affair with Kamal Kareem Moorehead, because she was in the habit of making suggestive asides about the "rhythm" of black men, and she didn't mean dancing. She would make these remarks in front of Bobby Bose, who was too stupid to realize what was going on, and she would pay little or no attention to my warnings that if she persisted, her eighth-grade-educated husband would someday catch on—and one day he did. He got out of bed one morning and found on the sheets beneath him little curls of hair too tight and too kinky to be his own. He knew his pubic hair like the back of his hand (and, I imagine, the back of his hand knew his pubic hair rather well and rather frequently, given my sister's diminishing interest in his penis), and he knew the pubic hair in the bed that morning was not his. It was black, first of all. Bobby Bose was a dirty blond. And there were way too many ringlets. His pubic hairs were undefined, stray, inconsistent curls. These were too perfect, too circular, too consistent.

The divorce was quick but ugly. There were violent words but no violent actions. And yes, there were threats. My parents tried to pay Bobby to shut up and leave the state, but the unfortunate subject of tea in China reared its Asian head again and thus another battle ensued, ending with the aforementioned threat from Bobby that he would get revenge.

I suppose one might say that, yes, in fact, Bobby had succeeded. With revenge, that is. He posed naked, stretched across the hood of his El Camino, and sold the photos to *Playgirl.* The spread was called "No More Feeding the Meter," and it scandalized my parents and their empire for a moment or two and then went away. Bobby had the IQ of a toothpick, but he was as good-looking as any dumb cowboy I've ever seen. Dreamy blue eyes and dimples to die for. And he had a very big dick.

No, I never made a pass at him. I would never sleep with my sister's man, no matter how handsome, no matter how well-endowed, no matter that he could shoot his load down the hallway and out the front door (this, Chaka later told me, was a great feat, but not quite as important as "rhythm"); besides, I had a policy of never sleeping with any man who couldn't spell the word *ejaculate*. I did meet a man once on Halloween who spelled it "ejaculantern," and I gave him extra credit for being timely, topical, and creative, and we made mad passionate love dressed as Darth Vader and Obi-Wan Kenobi.

I'm going back to the Vineyard in the morning. I don't have time to convince Chaka about anything. While she is busy trying to convince the Urban League that she too is African-American, I will be on-island checking every register in every guesthouse, motel, hotel, and resort for bookings during the week Father was killed. I will be looking for the name Bobby Bose.

Ten

Most of my friends are on antidepressants. Not my best friend, Stevie. He's just a happy guy with a cell phone. We often talk about the state of our generation; we are, after all, a horse with no name, a tribe without a homeland, an orchestra without a pit. We have no identity. We are thirty. We are thirty-three, thirty-four, thirty-six, and thirty-nine, and we are looking back and wondering what the hell happened. How come nobody gave us a topic?

Stevie and I often try to pinpoint the very onset of this collective malaise, the very moment we knew the rut as a rut, and the reasons for the rut become ever more clear.

Recession.
Layoffs.
Corporate greed.
MSG.
Steven Seagal.
AIDS.
Studio apartments.
E-Coli.
Gangsta rap.
Air pollution.
Noise pollution.
Water pollution.
George Bush.
Both of them.

Famine.
Blight.
Cancer.
Crack cocaine.
Arrogance.
Bowling.
The Gulf War.
Fried dough.
Friends.
Women who love...
Too much.
And the men...
Who hate them.
Tom Green.

Pamela Anderson.
Managed care.
Mismanaged care.
Made-for-TV movies.
Jerry Springer.
Cost of therapy.
"Talk to the hand..."
Mad cow disease.
Taxes.
Death.
Taxes.
Kathie Lee Gifford.
Kelly Ripa.
Bad bosses.
Bad excuses.
Bad sex.
No sex.
Right-wing fanatics.
Home Improvement.
Congress.
"Don't go there."
Alpha males.
Avoiding the Noid.
Tax-and-spend liberals.
The Patriot Act.
Supersize fast food.
Anna Nicole Smith.
Velveeta.
Rape.
Murder.
Grunge.
Jared from Subway.
Martha Stewart.
Interns.
Jesse Helms.
Reality TV.
Bumper stickers.
Homelessness.
Joblessness.
The Osbournes.
Geraldo Rivera.
Closets.
Paula Jones.
Viagra.
Global warming.
Ron Popeil.
Overpaid athletes
The Macarena.
The Thigh Master.
Bronson Pinchot.
O.J. Simpson.
Susan Smith.
Lickmyass.com.
El fucking niño.

We made it that far down the list when I heard "Attention Kmart Shoppers..." in the background.

"Where are you calling from?" I ask Stevie.

"Kmart."

"Oh. I thought I was hearing things."

"You weren't."

"Are you shopping for something?"

"I'm in the patio furniture department."

"You have patio furniture. Very nice patio furniture, if I do say so myself."

"I'm resting. Not really shopping."

"Resting? On the patio furniture?"

"Exactly."

"You're just sitting there on a chaise lounge chatting on the cell phone?"

"I'm not sitting. I'm almost fully reclined."

"Oh?"

"I was in the middle of shopping. I got tired. I saw a place to rest. I got lonely and I thought I'd call."

"I'm leaving for the Vineyard in a few hours. Want to come?"

"You're going back?"

"Yeah. Have to..."

"Bobby Bose?"

"You think I'm crazy, don't you?"

I hear his hesitation exhaling in nervous sighs through the phone line.

"You do, Stevie. You think I'm nuts."

"No, I don't. I support you fully..."

I'm not convinced. "You're just saying that to appease me. Do you think I need Prozac?"

"Prozac?"

"All of our friends are on it."

"No," Stevie says with a little fetching laugh, "you don't need Prozac."

"Zoloft?"

"No, Gray. Now stop this. I understand your Dad's death is still haunting you—"

"You can say that again. Especially after that séance."

"And I understand that this quest of yours to free your mother and apprehend the real killer is suddenly taking over your life, but come on, Gray, be your own best friend, my man, be good to yourself, don't let your imagination imprison you."

My eyes start to trickle a bit. This is what it means to have a true best friend. "I only tell you these things 'cause you're my hero."

He snickers. "Stop it, you queer."

"You can call me that because I love you. But I'm serious. I can tell you things because you're the healthiest friend I've got."

"Attention Kmart shoppers..."

A pause, a jumble of feet, other voices. Finally, "Shit, Gray, I got to go."

"Someone wants to buy the chair?"

"Yes."

"Then get the hell up and come with me to the Vineyard."

"All right, all right, already. Meet me at the airport. We'll take the *Luftpussy.*"

That's his plane.

"I was planning on taking the ferry."

"Takes too long. I'd rather fly," Stevie says.

"Okay."

Stevie Goldman and I have been best friends for eighteen years, since our freshman year at college.

The circumstances were odd, yet curiously maneuvered by fate and fellatio. My freshman-year roommate, a giant gentile named Patrick McPherson who played all kinds of sports and made half-Jews like me feel almost as inferior as total Jews, had an incredibly athletic appetite for sex. His first girlfriend was a coed named Deidre O'Connor who behaved as though she had just discovered her vagina. They were destined for combustible sex. And marathon fellatio. I woke one morning to odd moans and groans, light, lilting sighs, and a slurping sound that was consistent in rhythm and timing. I looked over to Patrick's bed and saw something shaped like a ball going up in down over his groin area. It was upon further inspection that I discovered the ball-shaped object to be Deidre's head under the blanket, busy at work on what had to be her first real-life penis.

I left the room.

I went back an hour later.

Moan, groan, slurp.

I left the room.

I wandered around the dormitory. I passed by open doors and waved hello.

I heard music ranging from Bruce Springsteen to Ella Fitzgerald, from Elvis Costello to Bob Dylan, from Julie Andrews (gay student) to the Grateful Dead (future drug supplier).

I returned to my room at nightfall.

Moan, groan, slurp.

A bit labored by this point, but *moan, groan, slurp* nonetheless.

I went to the laundry room and started folding strangers' clothes that had been left in the dryers. I came across lots of men's underwear, which kind of made me horny, considering the scene I had witnessed on and off all afternoon in my dorm room, and I was tempted to...well, never mind that. Suffice it to say I took just a little extra time folding the men's underwear, letting my imagination run wild and my cock grow to proportions I only thought possible among the girthiest Catholics.

"Excuse me...but I think you're folding my clothes."

I laughed.

He didn't.

I apologized and explained my predicament.

"Lucky guy, your roommate," the young man said. We shook hands. He said his name was Stevie Goldman. He smelled faintly of Lagerfeld. He said he lived one flight up and I could camp out in his room if this suckathon went on any longer.

Stevie is a handsome guy. He's from Arizona and has a certain desert sparkle in his eyes, a laid-back bliss in his smile. His hair is golden like the desert sun, his skin bronze like the bare skin of mountains at dusk. Stevie is not gay. Had he been, we might have started a suckathon all our own. But as soon as we returned to his dorm room he introduced me to his girlfriend, a lovely Hawaiian woman named Martina whom he had met on the subway in downtown Boston on her way to a class at B.U. Law School. Yes, she was quite a bit older than Stevie, but that didn't seem to pose a problem. Until much later in the semester when she confessed that she was actually kind of seeing someone else who was also studying law. Actually, she was kind of married to the guy. It broke Stevie's heart, but he was brave.

Martina and Stevie slept quietly that night with me in the room. Knowing what I had been through, they were kind enough to show restraint. I think I caught Stevie touching Martina's nipple once that night, but when he saw me eyeing him he simply shrugged and passed me an impish "it's only a nipple" smile.

The next morning I returned to my room.

I walked right over to Patrick's bed, ripped the blankets off of Deidre's head, and found her swollen lips still embracing my roommate's penis.

"My God, Deidre! Your mouth is going to freeze like that!"

She scampered from the room.

Stevie, waiting outside in the hallway, burst into tears, he was laughing so hard.

I knew I had a friend for life.

Stevie designs big buildings. He likes to dream them up from the sky. That's why he got his pilot's license after his first big break with an architectural firm in Boston. I didn't approve (of the license, not the firm), because I once bet him *Entre Tetas* that I would die first, not him, and that he'd be carrying my casket, not me carrying his. We were stoned at the time. But it was a bet I didn't intend to lose.

He calls the plane *Luftpussy* because, he says, flying is better than sex. I have told him many, many times that the name is disgusting and it's just one more reason why I hate to fly with him, but this never dissuades him, and what I really think is that Stevie has some major issues around intimacy (especially after Martina) and has replaced women with his plane. Vagina, cockpit—same difference.

"Cessna Titan, N-7404, cleared for landing."

Stevie is too young to be flying such a luxurious plane. Twin engine. Eight reclining supple leather seats. But he's doing quite well for a thirty-seven-year-old architect, so who am I to begrudge his indulgences, extravagant though they may be. Who am I but an heir to a parking-meter empire who in the meantime counts condoms for a living? Well, that's how it feels, you know, having been banished from my family's company. But I'm not bitter. And I'm not on antidepressants. Not yet, anyway.

"Do you want to land this one?"

I look at Stevie like he's crazy. "What are you, crazy?"

He laughs. "No, Gray. I'll guide you. I have the controls as well."

"No, thanks."

"Aw, c'mon. Live a little." Then, "Tower, this is Cessna Titan N-7404 on final approach. One passenger. A big wussy named Graydove."

☽

We rent a car at the airport.

I remove a notebook from my briefcase and flip a few pages until I find my list. "We'll hit all the hotels and guesthouses in Oak Bluffs, Vineyard Haven, and Edgartown today. The rest I'll get on my next visit. Unless you want to spend the night at *Entre Tetas*."

Stevie pretends not to hear.

"You're afraid," I tell him.

"What? Afraid of what?"

"Of my haunted house."

He laughs a fake laugh and knows I know it's fake.

"Here," I point at my lists. "We'll divide up the places in each town. And we'll split up, okay?"

"Sure, Gray. Whatever you want."

I truly love Stevie Goldman. That's why he's still my best friend on the planet. I'm not attracted to him anymore, haven't been for God knows how long (though I'd prefer to think that God has better things to worry about), and I can tell him things I can't even tell Pedro (mostly because they're things about Pedro), and we have this remarkable relationship that makes me feel like he's the brother I never had—besides Kirkland (like I said, the brother I never had). So that's probably why I don't covet his nakedness against my own; it would be like incest.

Oak Bluffs looks sad and lonely under this gray autumn sky. The streets are blackened by a recent rain. Most places are closing for the season.

There is too much space between cars.

It is so quiet I can hear my heartbeat echo in my ear canal.

I go one way. Stevie goes the other.

I fail at my first stop. They won't release the information I'm looking for. Their registration is private and confidential. What if someone had checked in to have an affair? What then? That's not the scenario they presented to me, but clearly it was the implication.

The next guesthouse was no more agreeable. "Look, Gray," they told me. "We're terribly sorry about what happened to your father. He was a good man. But you're wasting your time."

No, I wanted to tell the Slaters, who could only marginally claim to know my family (Mother and Father would occasionally book guests into the Slater by the Sea Guest House when *Entre Tetas* was full to capacity with overnight visitors and other hangers-on), *you* are wasting *my* time.

Two hotels, two dead ends. No one wanted to help. Sure, they all said they'd *love* to help, but really they just couldn't, not without jeopardizing the privacy of their guests.

Stevie walks toward me with his head hanging low. His shoulders are bent, his hands in his pockets. Apparently he's had no more success than I. He feels like he's let me down. He doesn't have to say it. I can see it in his eyes.

He shakes his head.

"No luck," I say.

He shakes his head again.

"Don't feel bad. Me neither."

"Edgartown?"

"Sure," I say. "Edgartown."

The proprietors of hotels and guesthouses in Edgartown *really* want to help us. But they can't. They feel *really* bad. But not bad enough to hand over the registration books. They suggest going to the police. The same police who put Mother in jail. They must be joking. They don't seem to be. They actually seem quite serious, which makes me shake my head in disbelief and want to walk off some not-so-distant pier.

"Vineyard Haven?" Stevie asks.

"Fuck Vineyard Haven," I say. "It's gonna be the same shit there."

My better judgment must have popped out of my asshole during some momentary turbulence on *Luftpussy*'s flight over here, because I sense an idea coming at me like a one-night stand I know I should get out of. One on hand it's tempting and arousing and seems like a good thing. On the other, it's rather repulsive to consider fucking the butthole of a total stranger or, in this case, paying a visit to the Voodoo Lady, Brenda Cloudholder. I should, but I shouldn't. I know better, but I don't.

❩

"Hello, Graydove! What brings you here?"

The hand closest to the butthole usually wins.

She welcomes us into her home. There are lots of small lamps and shadows. The light seems blue. The walls are dark wood, and I hear Lourdes meowing her brains out.

Brenda allows Lourdes to guide all of us into a small sitting room where books line the walls and plants dangle from the highest shelves. Lord only knows how she waters them, but then, of course, I remember Derderva and wonder where the gangly creature might be. Probably gone home for Halloween to visit his family (Morticia, Gomez, Lurch).

Lourdes farts.

I wonder if this isn't really a problem. I'm about to suggest perhaps a different kind of cat food, but Brenda gets the first word.

"You're back to hunt for your father's killer."

"Yes," I say. "You must be psychic."

Stevie snickers.

"No, dear," Brenda says, undaunted by my sarcasm, "it's easy to see the desperation in your eyes."

I cough. I stutter. Then I just fucking say it: "But Brenda, you're blind. How can you see anything in my eyes?"

"I sense it," she says.

"Of course you do." I've heard all about blind people with superior senses. But come on, I'm searching for my father's murderer...what's the chance there'd be anything in my eyes other than desperation? Lust, maybe? Joy? An eyelash?

Okay, for whatever reason, I came here. I peel the layer of cynicism from all *my* senses, and I try to welcome the woman's spiritual gifts into my life, if for only this once, and because it appears to be free.

"Can you help us?" I ask. I explain our fruitless efforts to track Bobby Bose to the island at the time of Father's death.

"And why are you so sure it's him?" she asks.

"I'm not. But he's as much a suspect as anyone else. Maybe more so, because he had a motive."

I describe how Bobby Bose had threatened father's life.

There's a heavy silence. And then Brenda Cloudholder lets out a deep breath. "Your father was right about the tea in China."

I'm confused and, I have to admit, bemused. She's either ten steps behind me or ten steps ahead. The fun of it, I see, is finding out. "I just want to rule him out. Then I'll know. And if it's not him, I'll look elsewhere."

She's smiling. "Now you're talking like a good detective."

I study the room's architecture. Books everywhere. "I guess you'd know detectives well. You've got plenty of crime novels here."

"Maybe you'd like to borrow some. Study up," she suggests cheerfully.

Again I hesitate. I fidget in my seat. "Well, I assume they're all in Braille...I don't know that I'd understand very much."

"They're not in Braille," she tells me. There is no irony in her voice.

"Let me guess...Derderva reads to you?"

She shakes her head. "No, dear. Lourdes does."

Stevie lets out a sudden laugh, a burst that, had his mouth had been full, would have pushed out projectiles of food.

I step on his foot. Hard.

Lourdes lets out another puff of kitty gas.

Stevie is turning purple. I have no doubt that Brenda is on to all of this. I compose myself. "We really need to know who was on-island at the time of Father's death."

"Why don't you just ask your father?"

"You mean...?"

"You know what I mean."

"No, Ms. Cloudholder. Not another séance. I was thinking of something more earthly. Perhaps you know some innkeepers on the island. Maybe you could run interference for me."

"I keep to myself."

I grimace. "But you've lived here forever, haven't you?"

"I like to think so."

"And you do have clients here, don't you?"

"Of course."

"And some of them must be connected to tourism here. I mean, everyone is somehow connected to the summer season."

"True," she says, with a sweet voice but a terse face. "But my client list is confidential."

"I'll pay you four thousand dollars."

Her face turns sweet, her voice terse. "Five," she says. "Five thousand."

I mull it over. *Five thousand dollars! What am I, crazy?* "Will you take a check?"

She smiles.

Stevie rolls his eyes.

I flash him a what-the-fuck look. What the fuck am I supposed to do?

He shakes his head.

I turn my hands up in the air, like I am juggling a question mark in each.

"Oh, Graydove, how your father loved you so..."

"What?"

"Your father. He adored you."

"Really?"

"Yes. Really. You act as if you didn't know."

My body is warmed. I feel a light on me that I can't explain. "Well...I mean, I knew he loved me...but...I guess I never heard it expressed like that."

She rises from her chair. "You will, Gray. You will."

I hand her the check.

"One of my most frequent clients runs the Steamship Authority," she says.

Saliva is already swirling down the insides of my cheeks. "And...?"

"And I'm sure I can make something work for you. He has all the records of everyone who has made the crossing since he took over some twenty years ago."

"That's a lot of paperwork."

"Insurance, my dear. It's such a litigious society we live in. People have faked going overboard."

"You're kidding!"

"I'm not," she insists. "I'm sure I can get access to last year's passenger lists. And we'll just see if Bobby Bose and his wretched El Camino came over to the island any time last summer."

My eyes grow wide, though I'm very self-conscious of looking surprised. "How'd you know he drove an El Camino?"

"I just know things."

I'm skeptical. This is a woman who is guided by a cat's meow...and I'm supposed to believe all this hocus-pocus. "But what if he didn't come over on the ferry?" I ask.

"You think he swam?"

I offer a contained laugh. "No, of course not. But he might have come by private boat, or by plane."

"Then I guess we'll have to check the airport records...and the Harbormaster at the marinas."

"They're your clients too?"

"Perhaps..."

I raise an eyebrow. Maybe two. "More money?"

"No, Gray," she replies. "I don't want more money. I can't help you with the airport or the Harbormaster. But Derderva can. If you're nice to him, that is. I sense you don't like him much."

I blush, then realize she can't see my redness, and it fades. "Well, no, I wouldn't say that..."

"I would," she insists. "I can sense it."

I consider her blindness again, and the power of her other senses. "Yes, I suppose you can."

She pats me on the back—once Lourdes leads her there—and directs me to the door.

Stevie takes the hint and follows.

"Derderva's ex-wife runs the airport. They're on extremely congenial terms. I'm sure she'd be happy to help," Brenda says as the screen door shuts behind me. I turn and stare at her through a million intersections of wires. A shadow of the grid lands on her face and she looks oddly like a jigsaw puzzle. "And his son, Willy, works on the Harbormaster's boat."

"A family dedicated to transportation," I say as I nod my head and back away.

She says nothing, just looks at me with her blind eyes; Stevie shakes his head.

☽

We ascend into the sky above the Vineyard.

"You're nuts," Stevie says, "and she's nuts. But I'm more worried about you."

I groan. "Please don't give me a hard time about this," I beg. "I feel I made some progress today. I see this as moving forward."

"Forward?"

"Just play along, Stevie. I need support right now. Not second-guessing."

"I'm sorry."

"No, it's okay."

"Really, I'm sorry."

He banks hard to the right. The island slants, and for a moment it looks miraculous that the ocean doesn't spill right over. Everything hangs precariously at this globe-tilting angle. "Don't be, Stevie. I'm not so sure about this myself."

He levels the airplane. We fly over my favorite part of the island. The outermost part.

"I love Gay Head," Stevie muses.

"So do I. So do I."

Yes, I am laughing inside, even at this, a joke so old on the Vineyard nobody mentions it anymore. But Stevie is quite serious. He loves Gay Head. He has no idea what he has said. And that makes it even funnier. To me.

"Look!" he cries. He sounds like a child on board a plane for the very first time. I love this about him.

"What?"

"That's her house! We were just there."

I lean forward and crane my neck toward Stevie's side of the cockpit. I'm not sure what he's seeing. But then he banks a bit sharper and there it is—in perpendicular salute—Brenda's house.

"Yes," I say, hoping my acknowledgment will persuade Stevie to level the plane from this particularly daunting pitch. "That's her house, all right. Keen, those eyes of yours."

We level. "Got to have good eyes to be a pilot."

"Yes, or a seeing-eye cat," I say, hiding my white knuckles under my lap.

We circle, and I can make out almost every shingle in Brenda Cloudholder's home. The place is weathered, but for some reason the shingles still look very precise.

"What's she doing?" Stevie asks just as I make out the figure of a woman on the lawn below.

"I don't know."

How odd. She's down there flailing her arms in the wind. She spins around in a circle. Her hands look like they're trying to sculpt the air.

"Maybe it's a blind thing," I say.

"Or a witch thing."

"Don't fly too low," I warn my friend. "I don't want to invade her privacy."

He ignores me and dips lower.

"Jeez, I don't think that's her," my pilot says. "I don't think that's your Brenda lady."

I squint and peer below. Stevie's right. It's not Brenda Cloudholder dancing down there across the lawn of sand and high yellow grass.

It's Derderva.

In a dress.

Eleven

Many weeks have passed since that visit to Brenda Cloudholder. By many I mean three. I haven't heard from her. Pedro has been gone the same amount of time. I haven't heard from him either. I hope he hasn't been charmed back into that Santeria business (not that there's anything wrong with it, he's just never the same after he's beheaded a couple of chickens). I tried calling twice. Both times I got his mother on the phone. Maria Elena Jimenez (they call her Mariel) told me he was out on the island and she didn't know when he'd return. This is what she told me both times. Both times she sounded all right. All right, that is, when you consider her son had rushed home for some kind of family crisis. Perhaps having Pedro there (when he wasn't *en la isla*) has been a comfort to her. I don't know. She offered to send me some *pasteles* ("You like my *pasteles, mi hijo,* don't you?"); I told her not to go to the trouble, she can just send some back with Pedro ("Do you know when he's coming back?"). She said no, she doesn't know ("*Ay, Dios mio, es un hombre diferente...*"). I take that as a compliment; it appears I've had a good effect on her son.

She blows me a kiss ("*un besito, mi amor*") through the phone. I blow her one back.

My boss walks by and gives me a curious smile. He doesn't say anything, but despite the gold band around his finger I think he might want a kiss blown his way as well.

King Products is showing a healthy profit. The books

are a joy to balance. Seems like everyone is using a condom. Except Chaka. I found out this morning on the way to work. We met at a diner. She looked green. Her cheeks were puffy.

"I'm pregnant with Kamal's child," she told me.

You idiot is all that came to mind.

"Say something, Gray."

I was speechless.

"Gray?"

"You're forty years old. Is it safe?"

"What?"

"Is it safe?"

She tossed me a look of disgust so physical, so tangible, so animate that I might have actually caught it had my hands not otherwise been occupied forking and knifing their way through a pair of cheese blintzes (melt in your mouth, to die for). "You *know* it's safe. You *know* women can have babies into their forties now without a problem. That's not your real concern. You're upset by the idea of me having a black man's child!"

"Upset? Who said I was upset?"

"You look upset. You sound upset. I think you're upset."

"Believe it or not Chaka, this isn't about *you,*" I told her. "I do have things on my mind. But they don't happen to be about the biracial embryo nesting in the cobwebs of your womb."

"You're an asshole."

"You came here looking for a fight, Chaka. Why don't you just admit it? I'm the only one of your siblings you love enough to get in a row with."

"*Row?* That's *très* continental..."

"I get it from Mother."

"Have you gone to see her lately?" Chaka asked with a trace of acquiescence in her voice.

"No. I should, though."

"So should I. Meet me after work. We'll go visit. We can tell her together."

"Tell her what?"

"That's she's going to have a mixed-race grandchild."

"But if you're truly black, Chaka, the baby won't be mixed-race after all."

She stopped in mid chew. "I suppose you're right, cracker."

I rolled my eyes. "Besides, we're all mixed. We've got the genes of Jews, Indians, and all the white people who oppressed them."

☽

I pass by my boss's office. His name is Ben.

"Good night, Ben."

He nods, waves a hand, and smiles.

He wants to lick my ass, I just know it!

Sometimes you just know certain things. I smile back and feel so sorry for his wife, a TV anchorwoman who is very popular among Boston viewers and apparently unaware that her husband is a homo. I've met her. She's a fun gal. She has fellatio-full lips and twinkling eyes. She has no illusions about being a journalist, having eschewed college for the beauty pageant circuit. She's won a few crowns.

"The viewers don't seem to care," she's told me. "As long as my hair looks good, nobody complains."

"Sad," I stated. "But probably true."

I've noticed that her hair is not her only asset.

She has very large breasts, which she seems to employ in her delivery of the news. While most anchorpeople emphasize certain words by bobbing their heads up, down, back, forth, side to side, Marla Cunningham shimmies her shoulders and shakes those mammaries of hers as if she is *heaving* the news to her audience.

"Oh, Gray...?" Ben calls to me from the doorway of his office.

I turn to him, images of his bosomy wife still fresh in my mind. "Yes?"

"I have a favor to ask..."

Ben asks a lot of favors. "What is it?"

"Can you give me a lift to the airport next Friday? Marla's busy, and I'd rather not take a car service."

I wince. "Yeah, sure. Just remind me."

"I sure appreciate it, Gray."

I turn and continue my exit.

Ben is not much older than me. He may be forty, but I doubt it. He has a baby face. He tries to hide it behind his professorial eyeglasses and his serious posture. He has golden hair that is always styled just right, professionally parted, but playfully loose and unsprayed. He wears suspenders always and a yuppie grin most of the time. He is impressed with himself and the car he drives (Lexus). He smells like Calvin Klein on Mondays, Aramis on Tuesdays, Halston on Wednesdays, Nautica on Thursdays, and Polo on Fridays. I am paying too much attention. But then my penchant (read: *obsession*) for the right colognes at the right time and the right place should be very clear by now.

Ben is six foot two.

Weighs two hundred pounds.

Looks great in a suit. Better in jeans (seen that twice).

Ben is a fine-looking man.

☽

The elevator sucks me down to the ground and Chaka is standing there, her pregnant self, waiting for me in the lobby.

We drive to Framingham practically in silence. Occasionally she fidgets in her seat in some vain attempt, I assume, to get my attention and draw some communication from me. It fails. I still think she's an idiot. I don't care if the baby is half-white, half-purple. I don't really care that this baby is coming as Chaka's biological clock strikes midnight. I care that Chaka's news is going to devastate Mother. Celeste Garrison Hoffenstein is not ready to be a grandmother. There's not enough plastic surgery in the world to reverse *that* sign of aging. Besides, "Over the river and through the woods, to Grandmother's jail we go..." just doesn't have quite the same ring to it.

The Massachusetts Correctional Institute at Framingham is a women's prison that looks like an old asylum—haunted by crazy souls and their dark wails of agony. It is red brick that always looks like it has been rained on. It is large and imposing and surrounded by razor wire that reminds me, every time I see it, of hemorrhoids.

I don't much like the place.

I cried for days after my mother was sentenced.

I could have handled her being sent away from us. Tasmania, for example. But the thought of my elegant mother surrounded by tough, terrible women who don't know the difference between mutual funds and mutual masturbation, between bud vases and Bud Light, between diamonds and cubic zirconia, was taxing on my sensitive soul and tender heart.

I still cry sometimes.

"Two visitors for Celeste Garrison Hoffenstein," I announce.

"Two for CeCe!" the manly woman yells to another uniformed guard...er, corrections officer. They liked to be called corrections officers. They've told me.

The announcement echoes down the prison chamber of metal doors and bars and locks and jangling keys. "Two for CeCe?"

CeCe? Where the hell did she get that winner of a name?

Mother appears. Her lips are well-glossed. Her eyes are made up, her fingernails freshly polished. Still, my heart drops into my stomach. Even with all the cosmetic attempts otherwise, and despite her unlikely age for incarceration,

Mother has acquired *the look*. She is hardened. Toughened. Let's face it (and I, of all people, should know better), she has the jail-made-me-a-lesbian look.

I don't know what to say.

She picks up on this. And being the mother that she is and hopefully always will be, she takes it upon herself to make the first difficult move. "Hello, children," she says. "You both look terrific. I'm delighted to see you."

I want her eyes to fill. They don't. I want her chin to quiver. It doesn't. When she first went to jail and we would come and visit, Cele would always cry on cue; she would collapse into our arms and tell us we were "her babies" and how badly she needed us. She would smother us with kisses, her heaving breasts pummeling against us as she sobbed and gasped for air. We would let her cradle us for the entire visit if she needed to.

She doesn't need to anymore.

I don't know what to make of that. So I just lean forward and give her a kiss and say, "Mother, how are you doing?"

Her answer is slow in coming. Her eyes are studious, but the study is a mystery. Her eyes are fixed on something beyond the prison walls. I am aware of a distance between us. "I'm doing just fine," she says. "Would you like to see something I made in pottery class?"

I fear my speech will turn to stutter. I simply smile and offer an emphatic nod. Yes, I'll go along with this sad metamorphosis. I smile and nod again.

"Mother is there anything you need?" Chaka asks. "Anything we can do to make this place more bearable for you?"

"I want you both to start visiting Father's grave regularly."

This is the first time she has mentioned Father since she's been incarcerated.

"I need you to do that for me," she continues. "I realize now that I never had a chance to grieve."

"And that's so important, Mother," Chaka tells her.

"You don't know how important. In the past year, since the murder, all I could do was think of the trial. I had to think strategy. I had to think possibilities. I had to plan for two different outcomes. I don't expect you kids to understand. But my period of mourning was stolen from me."

My eyes begin to fill. My chin begins to quiver. I put my arms around my mother and hold her tight. My tears drip into the scoop of her neck and shoulder. She puts a hand on my head and runs it through my hair. "Anything we can do to help you grieve Mother, we will. Anything," I tell her.

She takes my face in her hands and she brings it to hers. "You be my conduit to Father. You be my messenger."

"Thank you for asking," I say.

Chaka brushes her lips softly against our mother's cheek. "We will put you in touch with Father. We've already contacted a medium."

"Brenda Cloudholder?"

"Yes."

"Your father used to talk a lot about her. He had hoped she could communicate with some of his Indian ancestors."

"She's expensive," Chaka says tentatively.

"Money's no object. You kids know that. Those godforsaken parking meters just keep the coins rolling in." Cele laughs at that one. Amused at herself for taking her riches, perhaps for the first time in her life, not so seriously.

When we ask to see the pottery a while later, she balks at the request with a dismissive wave of the hand. "That was a front, an icebreaker, a simple, uncomplicated thing for me to talk about," she admits. "I was afraid my grief for Father would be too much for you to take. I was afraid of burdening you with it. I didn't know whether to say anything."

"We're glad you did," Chaka assures her. "But there may be something that's too hard for *you* to take."

Mother gives us that old Celeste Garrison Hoffenstein

look of curiosity. She arches her eyebrows like a wicked Spanish actress. Her lips get saucy and flirtatious with the idea of knowing something secret. This is such a relief. This glimpse of the Cele we knew, this fleeting visit to our life before IT happened, gives us back the winsome coquette that we call Mother.

Chaka tells her about the baby.

I'll be damned. Mother's eyes begin to fill. Her chin begins to quiver. She puts a hand to her heart. She is feeling love and loved.

We are silent until she is ready to speak, and when she does, she says simply, "If it's a boy, I'd be so proud if you named him Colin."

Chaka lifts her up into her arms. Both of them sob.

"Of course I will," Chaka promises. "I hope Father would be proud as well."

Sniffle. Sniffle. Cele dabs her eyes. "I know he would be."

Chaka's forehead creases. "But what if it's a girl, Mother?"

"Well, I hate the name Colleen," Mother tells us. "Loathe it, abhor it..."

Oh, she sounds so rich again!

"What about Colette?" I ask.

Both of them look at me with Joan Crawford looks of horror. The name "Colette" has stunk up the room like an old salami sandwich. Shit! The way they contort their faces and twist their mouths and whip their heads back, you would think I had asked them to *eat* an old salami sandwich. I realize this is a *woman* thing. After all, it's their womb, their cervix, their birth canal, their vagina that must stretch from here to the Continental Divide and back to let the baby out; surely they have the right to name it.

"We'll call her Colynn," Mother suddenly announces. "Colynn. C-O-L-Y-N-N."

"And if she's anything like her mother," I mutter not so

beneath my breath, "she'll change it to Kaleisha by the time she's seventeen."

But they are sobbing again, the name Colynn being so lovely and all, so they don't hear me, and I choose not to repeat myself.

Twelve

Skye is gushing, and I can almost feel the drools of excitement dripping through the receiver onto my face. I imagine my younger sister's black-as-ink curls all tangled as she throws her head back in a frenzy.

"It's a national commercial!" she cries. "National!"

"You mean for the rent-a-car place?"

She belts out a good laugh, a laugh that begs for, insists on, demands a co-conspirator. "No, Gray! A national commercial, as in I'm doing a commercial that will be seen nationally."

"Well, that's great!" I co-conspire. "What's it for?"

Her electricity seems to flatline. She is now sitting there, on her sofa, or at the side of her bed, maybe even smothered in a bathtub of foam, and she is feeding a strand of her wispy hair into her mouth. I just know this about her. "Well...it's for a feminine product," she says guardedly.

"A feminine napkin, you mean?"

"No."

"A feminine hygiene spray?"

"No."

"A douche?"

"No!"

"Panty hose?"

"No, not panty hose."

"Cross Your Heart Bra?"

"No. Cross my heart."

“I’m running out of things feminine, Skye. I’m running out of guesses.”

“Think vagina…”

“I’d rather not, sis. And it’s not because I’m a homo.”

She snickers. “Okay, fine, be that way. Make me tell you. It’s for a lotion to treat vaginal yeast infections.”

“Oh.” I’m aware of how underwhelmed I sound, and I try to muster something more. “Those are great spots! Really, they are! The women always look so relaxed, even though their cooters must be itching like moth-eaten wool.”

“Gray! That’s disgusting!”

“I’m sorry. I don’t know what to say.”

“Say you’re happy for me. Say you think it’s a great opportunity. Say anything. But don’t be so vulgar.”

“I’m happy for you. I think it’s a great opportunity. And you know what else, Skye? I think it shows you’re maturing. I think this could mean more work for you. You’re not being cast as a teenager anymore. And that’s good. You’re twenty-five…you should be playing at least twenty. I think these casting people are looking at you more seriously now as a *woman.*”

“I know. Isn’t it great?”

“It is,” I continue to co-conspire. “Now, when are you coming home from New York to visit Mother?”

“Mother?”

“Yes, Mother. You know, Celeste Garrison Hoffenstein?”

No answer.

“The one who pushed you through her birth canal with the force of a breaking dam, come hell or high water, yeast infection or not…?”

“I know who you’re talking about,” my sister tells me.

“I just thought you’re due for a visit. Chaka and I went a few days ago. We had news for Mother.”

“Oh?”

“But you’ll have to come to Boston to find out.”

"Stop that! I want to know now."

"Can't. It's not for me to tell."

"Well, a trip to Boston is out of the question. I've got contracts to sign, people to see, and God only knows when we're shooting this thing. I hope it's an L.A. job. I haven't been out to the coast for a while now."

"You're sounding like someone who actually earns a living from this acting and modeling..."

"What's that supposed to mean?"

"It means don't bite the hand that feeds the parking meter, Skye."

She grunts a laugh. "Very funny. I never take more than my share from the company. Just because they threw you out, don't blame me."

"We're not talking about me," I tell my sister. "We're talking about you and when the hell you're coming back here to visit Mother. I know she'd like to see you. She's putting up a brave front. But this family is everything to her. Everything. She'd gladly give up all the parking meters in the world to have this family back together again." I wince at my own words, for the thought of having my brother, Kirkland, in the same time zone appeals to me about as much as having an enema. Or giving one.

My appeal seems unappealing to Skye, as she simply says, "Enough, Gray. No more guilt trips. I'm twenty-five years old. I can make my own decision."

"So what is it?"

"I'll send her a clip?"

"A clip?"

"A clip of the commercial."

"You think these ladies all have VCRs in their cells, pumpkin? You think they have Video Night in the jailhouse?"

"Don't be ridiculous."

"Don't *you* be ridiculous, Skye. You haven't seen Mother in God knows how long, and your first contact with her is going to be a clip of you aching to scratch your pussy?"

"Vulgar, Gray, vulgar!"

"Deal with it, sis. I support you in your slow, dubious climb to stardom. But I think you need to give Mother back some of the love she's given to you."

Skye weeps softly into the phone. I am delighted, in a way. "I'll try, Gray. I'll try. Really, I'll do the best I can."

"That's all I wanted to hear," I say like a father. "Now, good luck on the commercial. And keep us posted."

"I will. You'll hear from me soon."

I'm lowering the handset when I hear Skye's voice calling me back.

"What?"

"Hey, Gray, have you been calling me lately and leaving Liza Minnelli songs on my answering machine?"

"What?"

"Liza Minnelli songs. Someone's been leaving them on my machine."

"Why would I do that?"

"I don't know. Just asking."

"You think just because I'm gay, 'New York, New York' is some kind of signature for me?"

"Well, now that you mention it..."

"Goodbye, Skye."

"Bye, Gray. And, hey, 'Start spreading the news...' " she roars like a Broadway diva.

"Start spreading your legs," I retort.

She slams down the phone, and I'm staring at the receiver in my hand, only slightly bewildered, when I realize Ben, my boss, is hovering over my shoulder, circling my desk like an airplane trying to land at O'Hare.

"Yes?" I ask politely.

"It's Friday. Did you forget?"

"Friday?"

"My ride to the airport," he says with a wink.

"Oh, shit! That's right!"

He pouts (or maybe I'm just imagining this) and says, "Well, if you've made other plans, I can take a cab."

"No, really. No need to do that. It just slipped my mind, that's all. When do you need to leave?"

"Twenty minutes."

"Shit. I lost track of the time."

He raises an eyebrow. "Personal calls have that effect."

I look away, saying "I'm sorry" in another direction.

He puts his hand on my shoulder and leaves it there. He gives me a squeeze. "I'm just kidding. You're one of the best workers here, Gray. You manage to work fast and stay in touch with all your friends and family. Nothing wrong with that."

He smells good. No, great. *Anteaus* by Chanel. Perfect for flying. I'm getting an erection. I hate myself for it. I push my chair closer to my desk.

"Well, you just let me know when you're ready to leave, and we'll take off."

Another squeeze. "Huh! I get it! *Take off!* Like an airplane taking off..."

Actually, my wording was incidental, unintended, but I don't have the heart to tell him. I do have a hard-on, but I don't have the balls to tell him that either.

I'm putting my work away, paper-clipping papers, pencil-sharpening pencils, hiding my woody, when the phone rings. I swear, I was just going to rip off another page of my Day at a Glance and curse Pedro for letting so many days, make that so many weeks, pass without as much as a phone call when, in fact, I realize it's him on the line.

"Pedro!"

"I can't talk long, Gray. I'm sorry, it's just—"

"Don't worry. I'm pleased to know you remember my name."

"Stop it. I haven't forgotten about you."

"Oh, yeah? What color are my eyes? My hair? How big is my cock?"

"*No jodas, hermano,*" he says.

"I'm not fucking with you, man. I'm serious. I am fucking pissed you haven't called."

"Maybe I got a reason."

"Care to share it?"

"Not now. You'll see for yourself when I get home. I'm just calling to say I need another week here. Two at the most."

I let out a puff of indifference. I'm really not indifferent. But hell if I'm going to let him think I'm so dependent on his sorry Puerto Rican ass.

"How's your family? Your mother sounded fine when I talked to her. Has the crisis ended?"

He laughs abruptly. "Yeah, she sounded great, all right. But the crisis has only just begun."

We say no more.

I hear squealing in the background. It sounds like the voices of schoolgirls all a-giggle in Spanish glee. And then I think I hear Pedro say "I love you" to me, followed by a click, and then the phone goes dead.

☽

We're stuck in the tunnel. I'm stressed. It must be showing. I look in the rearview mirror. It is. My jaw is tight, and my teeth are grinding like bad brakes, metal on metal.

"Relax, Gray. I built in time for this."

"You did?"

"Of course," he says with a lighthearted laugh that is comforting. "When have you ever driven to Logan without getting stuck in traffic?"

"Two A.M. on a Tuesday morning," I reply smartly.

"Drug runs to Miami not included."

He makes me laugh. But behind the laugh, a wince. "Do you already have your boarding pass?"

"Yes," he answers. "Stop worrying. My flight doesn't leave for two hours. We'll be at the airport in fifteen minutes. I guarantee it."

"Jesus, do you really believe it when the airline tells you to check in two hours early?"

"Yes."

"That's ridiculous. You travel enough to know better."

A chuckle. A boyish chuckle seeps through his sophisticated facade. "I know, Gray. But I'll tell you something that nobody...well, nobody," he pauses and frowns, "but my wife knows. So it's just between you and me. Doesn't become office gossip..."

He's waiting for an answer.

I nod my head emphatically. "Yes, of course. Just between us."

"I'm a nervous flyer," he confesses. "I sometimes get stomachaches before a flight. So if I arrive early, I have time to throw up before boarding."

"Don't worry. I won't spread that around. Does this happen all the time?"

"Every so often."

"How are you doing tonight?"

"Actually, not bad. Not bad at all. I think I'll be okay."

We reach the end of the tunnel, where we're greeted by dusk.

"Then what are you going to do with yourself for two hours?"

He smiles fiendishly. For all I know he could be a fiend. People have many sides. "You're going to park the car and come inside with me and have a drink."

"I am?"

"Well, yes. Surely you didn't think I was going to have you drive me to the airport and not offer you a drink or something..."

I shrug. "That's okay. It's really no problem. Don't feel you have to repay me."

"Are you in a rush to get somewhere?"

I think for a moment and wonder if I should make something up. But I can't. I'm not a good liar. That surprises me sometimes. I think I'm the type of person who should be a good liar. But I'm not. My tongue gets tied. My ears start to itch. And my hands start to twitch. Sometimes I even pass an innocent and hopefully innocuous cloud of gas. Because that risk alone, I do not lie. "Not really," I tell him.

"Fine, then. It's settled," Ben says, sitting solid now, looking straight ahead, quite satisfied with himself.

Lord only knows what he has in mind.

☽

Inside the terminal, the announcements ricochet off one another; flights arrive; flights depart; flights are delayed. Two pieces of carry-on items. In the overhead bin or under the seat in front of you. FAA this, FAA that; get your ass on the plane and shut the hell up.

Ben is going to the home office in Des Plaines, Ill. He'll fly into O'Hare. Lucky him. He has wandered off to study the departures screen that hangs from the soaring ceiling. He turns around, and he has a chipper expression as our eyes meet. "Well, it's on time, believe it or not. That gives us a little over an hour. Here, why don't we slip into the Ambassadors' Club, where it's quiet. I'm a member, so let's see if they treat me like an ambassador...heh-heh."

Heh-heh.

We are surrounded by others who are hoping to be treated like ambassadors as well. We find a small table in the far corner, affording us a view of the dark landing field, its grid of blinking lights like a tic-tac-toe of the gods. Occasionally a plane will sweep by, its proud logo all lit up as it taxis home. A *whoosh,* and a plane ascends. A *rumble, rumble, thud,* and a plane touches down. We watch and are quiet for a few moments. A cocktail waitress named Terri takes our order.

"Marla and I are breaking up," he announces; his words are so enunciated, so precise, the air is cut in half.

With both eyebrows arched I say, "Divorce?"

"Yes."

"No!" I feign surprise, as if I think theirs was a marriage meant to last.

"She's having an affair with Beau Lager," he tells me.

"The weatherman!"

"One and the same."

Yikes. Beau Lager is chiseled to perfection. Hollywood smile. NFL shoulders. Blow-dried hair. Blow-dried brain. They, Marla and Beau, make a perfect couple.

"I am so sorry," I say, trying to unpuzzle the thoughts reeking from my boss's face.

"I'm not," he confesses. "It would never have lasted. She wants too much glamour. She wants to be one half of a glamour couple. An accountant for a husband just doesn't cut it."

"You're better off without her," I recite easily.

"I suppose."

Later, I walk him to the boarding lounge. Neither of us sets off the metal detector at the security station. He leads the way through, waits for me, and we walk silently onward.

His flight begins to board, families with small children, children traveling alone, first-class and business-class passengers first. Invariably, an adult traveling alone in coach steps forward. He is told he has to wait until his row is called. His idea of class is to mutter "cunt" under his breath as he walks away from the woman collecting tickets at the gate. She looks familiar to me.

"I'm flying business," Ben says as he digs into the inside pocket of his coat for his ticket.

We drift toward the ticket-taker. Ben parks his wheel-it-on suitcase and sets down his briefcase. Before I realize what he's reaching for, he grabs me and pulls me close. He pushes his tongue inside my mouth. His kiss is hot and endless.

From the corner of my stunned eye, I see the flight attendant looking at me and winking. I realize why I recognize her. She's the same ticket-taker who witnessed my farewell kiss with Pedro a few weeks ago.

Ben lets me go. He's breathless. His face beams with exultation and relief. He looks like a lion who has just had me for dinner. All to himself. He lifts his briefcase from the floor, swings his wheel-it-on around, and disappears down the jetway. I don't remember if he says "goodbye" or "see you in a week" or whether, without a word, he just takes his new-found, vibrantly transformed, sexually awakened self and heads off proudly into the skies with the same sense of accomplishment he might feel after, say, landing a multimillion-dollar client.

The gate agent nudges me. "Way to go," she whispers. "Weren't you just here a few weeks ago with another guy?"

I lower my eyes shyly. "What are the chances of me kissing two different guys in front of the same stewardess?"

"Flight attendant."

"I'm sorry," I say. "I knew that."

"That's okay. At least someone knows how to get a man."

I smile at her fondly. "What do you mean?" I ask.

"No sex in weeks. Broke up with my boyfriend."

"Oh, dear, you'll find someone better," I assure her.

"Not until I get rid of this yeast infection."

"Oh."

She walks away. I am staring off into the place where she just stood, and I can see, off in the distance, the plane rolling backward from the gate. Ben is aboard.

I am in trouble.

Thirteen

When people enter my home they tend to gawk. It was not intended to be a showplace. But this is where Cele has sent all the art pieces and priceless rugs she has tired of in her many homes. I live in a duplex penthouse overlooking the Charles River. I know this is luxury, and I know I'm fortunate. But tons of cash and a view to die for means nothing, I promise you, when your father's dead and your mother's in jail.

Guests like the private lap pool on the terrace.

We heat it and enclose it in winter, and there is something quite magnificent about splashing around in chlorinated bliss while snow shakes from the sky in frigid fury around you. The workers will come tomorrow, I think, to reinstall the plexiglass enclosure. Winter is hiding around the corner, it seems. Just look north and you can almost see its gray skies seeping downward from Canada.

I would like to solve Father's murder by Christmas. Or Hanukkah. I can't imagine a better gift to Mother than freedom from jail.

The master bedroom has its own steam room and sauna.

I am often surprised that Pedro and I haven't yet had sex in either. It seems so obvious. We have fucked in the weight room, though.

Mother and Father never lived here. They bought the place thinking they needed a home base in Boston. Parking Meters of the World is based here, but they never moved into the penthouse; they kept a suite at the Ritz (the tea-in-China Ritz) year-round for their comings and goings. Walk about three blocks toward the river from the Ritz, take a left at Emerson College (check out the precious budding actors along the way; many of them will be homosexual), and travel down Beacon to Gloucester Street and you will find my home. For many years before they handed me the keys and the name of an Irish housekeeper, Mother and Father would let their distinguished guests stay at the Gloucester penthouse whenever one would jet into town. Those guests included business clients, entertainers, socialites, a duke, a duchess, a mistress, and a Greek heiress who used to pee on our carpet.

Three guest suites. Each with private bath. Each with bidet.

Of course, this all happened after the family was raised. Before the suite at the Ritz, before the Gloucester Street penthouse, there was the family home in Ipswich, a huge albatross of a Tudor built on a cliff overlooking the sea that I swear to this day is full of ghosts.

I thought every child had an ocean for a front yard.

I thought every child had a governess.

I thought every child was whisked away to his other mansion on Martha's Vineyard when Ipswich became too hot and sticky in July.

My parents, God bless them, never taught us we were different. I'm almost certain they carried on unaware, themselves, of their extravagances. Nice things cost money. Money was no object. They had nice things. They donated tons of money to charity. They hosted balls and concerts and auctions. They raised a lot of cash for total strangers.

Did I mention the private elevator?

The maid's quarters?

The original Dali?

I probably mentioned the Dali. It's a real conversation piece.

Our family was remarkably not dysfunctional. How's that for a change? Refreshing, don't you think? I think it comes from our Native American blood. In fact, I'm sure of it. My

Native American grandmother used to sit me on her lap and tell me stories about the gods, and these stories sounded like fairytales to me. She would chant them out, these stories, and I would follow the rhythm of her soul as she sweetly opened these magic doors into a world only known by spirit guides and ancient loved ones. I wish I had realized what treasures these stories were; I wish I had understood the richness and abundance of her wisdom. I wish I had written some of these stories down, but I did not, and all I can remember now is the softness of my grandmother's voice, the way her inflection suggested a simple tale when really she was taking you on a journey both mystical and timeless.

Her face seemed ageless to me. Her skin was smooth and bronze and smelled smoky when I kissed her. She wore her black hair very long, and sometimes I would wrap it around *my* head and pretend it was mine. She died when I was fourteen, but I was old enough to understand when she explained that she had married my grandfather, a Jew, because they had so much in common. So much had been taken away from their cultures, from their people, from their histories and their futures. I understood this, and it made me richer than any trust fund could. I understood that together they were one, forging ahead, to right a wrong, to love not hate, to think and do, to teach, to learn, to heal and to preserve, and to save the world.

I'm sitting here in my two-story living room staring out at my two-story view (which I have not had to die for), thinking about the ancestry of who I am and where I came from, and I feel a great sense of love, not loss.

Father will be grateful when I find his killer.

So will the people who created him and loved him and cherished him and are with him now trying to understand for themselves.

If Bobby Bose didn't do it, who did?

I have waited long enough. I reach for the phone and dial Brenda Cloudholder's number.

She tells me she's heard nothing yet from her client at the Steamship Authority.

"What about the Harbormaster and the airport?" I ask.

"Derderva is working on it, Gray. But these things take time...require a great deal of delicacy."

"Have you heard from him?"

"From who?"

"From Father?"

She chuckles pleasantly. "No, dear, your father doesn't just pop in for a visit from the other side, you know. I wouldn't say we're *in touch,* so to speak."

"Oh."

"I can try to contact him again for you, if you'd like."

I can hear the cash register go *ca-ching* with every syllable she speaks. "That won't be necessary, I don't think."

"Okay," she says gently. "But if you change your mind, I'll conduct another séance for free."

I change my mind very quickly. After all, I've paid the woman five thousand dollars and so far she has come up empty-handed.

❩

Stevie flies Chaka and me to the Vineyard the following morning.

"I can't believe you're doing this," he groans.

"Wait till you see what happens," I tell him. "I think it's nuts. But it's very colorful. Real entertaining."

Chaka throws up.

I hold my nose.

Stevie hands my sister a paper bag.

"Morning sickness," she mutters.

Stevie peers at the big blue sky ahead of him. "If it's just entertainment for you, Gray, why are you wasting your time with this trip?"

"I'm not wasting my time. Brenda needs to know I'm serious. She needs to understand the urgency. She needs to get the fucking information from the Steamship Authority or the Harbormaster or the fucking airport before Christmas or Hanukkah or I'll just have to resort to my other plan."

"Your other plan?" he asks.

"I may have to break Mother out of jail myself."

Stevie laughs.

"I'm serious. But forget I told you this, or you'll be an accomplice."

"Forgotten. But why Christmas or Hanukkah?"

"It's just a deadline I set for myself."

Chaka coughs, then gags, then pukes.

Her face is bone-white.

I tell her to put her head between her legs (I've heard that on the big airplanes before). She does, and she then pukes on the floor.

"How soon till we land?" I ask the pilot.

Stevie studies a few gauges, says something to someone in a control tower somewhere, and then waits for an answer. "Ten minutes," he finally tells me. "We'll be on the ground in ten minutes."

I spend the next ten minutes thinking about the questions I'll ask Father in the unlikely event that Brenda Cloudholder produces him.

Obviously, my first question is: Who killed you, Father?

Then: Why?

My other questions will include: Did you really adore me like Brenda said you did?

Did you love Mother as much as she loved you?

Have you run into anyone interesting up there? JFK? Natalie Wood? Einstein?

Luftpussy glides into the airport. We roll to the end of the runway, and Stevie turns us left. Is that Walter Cronkite standing outside the terminal building? He has a home here on the Vineyard. So does Billy Joel, I think. My parents once invited him to dinner at *Entre Tetas* (they called it Sea Valley on the invitation), but he never replied. I think they should invite Cronkite. Before he dies. Or then again, after. Now that *Entre Tetas* has opened its hearth to the spirit world, we might as well invite them all. I'd really like to bring back Natalie Wood and ask her what the hell happened.

It's not Cronkite. We're closer now. I can see better. The man is too small. Younger, I guess. And he's picking his ass. I don't think Cronkite picks his ass.

"Are you okay?" I ask my sister.

"I'm fine," she grunts.

We take a cab to *Entre Tetas.*

The Yugo is waiting.

☽

We sit around the same table as at the last séance. Brenda, Lourdes, Chaka, Stevie, and me. Derderva has gone off to run errands. I had hoped to ask about the lawn-dancing, but he got away too quickly.

The room is cool, the heat having not kicked in yet. I sense winter will hit out here on the islands first; there will be raw days with damp chills and lead skies. There will be people with smiles forced as though they fancy themselves warriors toughing it out here on the fringes of civilized life, so few of them, so many things closed.

Brenda lowers her head and whispers. A squeezing of hands rounds the table. The furnace below us somewhere begins to rumble. Brenda lifts her head back, and I can barely make out the moving of her lips. She isn't whispering, yet I sense that words are being delivered from her mouth. She is in conversation. That much I can tell.

The room is amber. We have a few candles lit. That would

explain the wavering shadows, the orange glow, the dusky sense of sun setting on the other side. Jesus.

Stevie looks up and smiles. I cast him an admonishing glance and a quick *shh* movement of my lips. I hope he can control himself. He laughs at everything and has a very childish streak, and what I worry about is that his giddiness can be very contagious; he often makes me wet myself.

Suddenly Brenda tosses her head about and opens her mouth wide. She raises her hands and says, "I've made contact."

"With Father?" Chaka asks.

"Hold on…wait a minute," she replies. "No, I'm sorry. False alarm. I got his voice-mail."

We say nothing.

She smiles. "Just a little séance humor."

Stevie snorts an aggravated snort.

Chaka kicks him under the table.

"I felt that," someone says. But I don't know who it is. I look up and Brenda is searching the room from behind her dark sunglasses.

"Who said that?" she begs.

No answer.

We all turn our heads to one another, squeeze our hands tighter, and share the tingly rush of something unbelievable.

"Come forward and speak…do not be afraid," Brenda tells the entity.

"I'm here," the visitor says.

"Welcome," Brenda chants.

Chaka repeats, "Welcome."

So do I.

Then Stevie. Reluctantly.

The visitor is a woman, I think. The voice is soft and frail, but sweet, sweet as honey, the way her words pour out so slowly and gently. "Colin does not want to talk today. He's sent me to deliver his message…"

My face cannot withstand the socket-wide amazement of my eyes. I feel I need to pinch myself, but I'm afraid to move. I'm afraid and mesmerized, stunned and overjoyed. This woman is my grandmother. Of course it's her! Why else would I be thinking of her lately? She knew all along I'd be coming to speak to her. "Grandma?"

"Gray..." Her voice wraps around my head, trailing, echoing, like the call of a bird flying circles near its home.

My eyes begin to fill. My heart pounds. My skin gooses, and I feel a tremendous love like I have never known before. "Grandma, I miss you. I miss your stories about the moon and the sun and the stars. I can't even remember how they went. But I remember how you told your stories with such pure love in your voice and beauty in your eyes."

"Stop sucking up, Gray," Chaka snaps at me.

The table shakes.

"Don't get Grandma mad," I warn my sister.

Brenda Cloudholder clears her throat and flashes my sister and me an ugly stare, which is quite an accomplishment for a blind person wearing sunglasses in a dark room. We are sufficiently put in our place and reluctantly relinquish control of the séance once again to our medium.

"Deliver the message," Brenda tells my grandmother.

The room feels icy, suddenly. Like someone just opened the door to a walk-in freezer.

"Gray, you must come back and visit with me again soon," my grandmother says. "But for now, my mission is simple."

"Yes," Brenda interjects. "Simple, indeed. We want to make this very easy for you, dear. Has Colin sent you with something specific to say? Something more than a greeting?"

"Of course."

"Can we ask how he's doing?" Brenda wants to know.

"He's doing fine, children. Just fine."

"Does he miss us?" I ask despite the sternness on Brenda's face.

"Of course he does. We all do."

"He sent you with a message?" Brenda reminds our visitor.

"Yes."

"And?"

"He says you're looking in the wrong direction."

"The wrong direction?"

"Yes."

"Did he tell you who his murderer was?"

"No. He isn't sure he can do that."

"Why not?"

"There are a lot of issues."

"There are *issues* in heaven?" I ask.

"Darling, Gray, people have issues everywhere."

"But we're his family," I protest. "He can tell *us,* can't he?"

"He'd like to, I'm sure. But I'm his mother and he can't even tell me. Like I said, there are issues. I know my son. I think things are complicated."

Brenda exhales an impatient breath and says, "Well, fine, then, deliver the message and we won't take any more of your time. We wouldn't want to keep you here any longer than you wish."

"Not to worry."

"You were saying Colin wants us to know we're heading in the wrong direction."

"Yes. He hasn't told me who murdered him. But he's told me who hasn't."

"Who hasn't?" Brenda coaxes.

"Bobby Bose."

"Bobby Bose?"

"Yes, that good-for-nothing son of a bitch my granddaughter married when she somehow lost her head."

Chaka shrieks.

Stevie belts out a good laugh.

I shake my head. "People talk like that in heaven, Grandma?"

"Heaven, shmeaven. It's a free-for-all, Gray."

"Wow."

The room is warm again. The light is natural, not opaque and shadowy anymore.

She is gone, but there is an urgent knock on the door, and I wonder, as I'm sure the others do, if Father has decided to show up after all.

But Father, of course, would not need to knock.

"Please let me in!" the voice calls from outside.

"It's Derderva," Brenda growls. "What the hell could that fool want? Let him in."

I do.

He rushes past me into the parlor. He flips on the lights, and the hands being held around the table unlock uniformly, like some kind of machine abruptly stopped.

"I got it!" he cries. "I got it!"

"What, Derderva?" Brenda demands. "What is so urgent that you interrupt this fragile connection with the other side?"

"I found something at the airport! He was here! I went through all the manifests from the flights last summer. His name was on one. Bobby Bose was here!"

We look at one another, dumbfounded.

"What?" Chaka asks.

"Bobby Bose was here the week your father was murdered."

Fourteen

Who do you believe? A Yugo-driving chauffeur seen on at least one occasion lawn-dancing in a dress? Or your grandmother's ghost?

We fly back to Boston in silence, each of us contemplating those questions, I imagine, in our own way. The silence would have been complete had it not been for the incessant banging coming from the right engine.

"I don't think it's the engine, Gray," Stevie tells me.

"Well, don't you hear the banging?"

"Of course I hear the banging, but I'm telling you it's not the engine."

"Whatever. Just tell me when to bail out."

My sister rolls her eyes. She's holding her stomach; I'm expecting her to throw up again. It would provide such symmetry to this trip of ours: puking coming, puking going.

She doesn't puke. She just holds her stomach. The banging (which, whether Stevie admits it or not, does come from the right engine) doesn't seem to bother her. She mumbles something about it being the big baby in the sky kicking at the stomach of God.

"Spare me," I beg.

One hundred and twenty-seven bangs later we land.

Stevie does a quick inspection of the plane and shrugs. "Everything looks normal."

"Do me a favor," I say. "Have your maintenance guy look at it. Just to be safe."

"Of course I will," he assures me. "And I'll have him check my indicators as well. Maybe there's something faulty there."

"Maybe."

Kamal Kareem is waiting for Chaka.

"Hello, father-to-be," I say with a grin (albeit shit-eating). "May I nominate you for Sperm of the Year?"

Kamal Kareem laughs and I notice, perhaps for the first time, his amazing dental hygiene (pearly white teeth and all that).

Stevie drives me home.

It's getting dark.

"I hope you don't drop Bobby Bose as a suspect, just like that," Stevie says with a crisp snap of his fingers.

"Who said I was?"

"No one, but I think you can trust information from a live source better than, well, a source from the spirit world."

"The whole séance thing turned you off."

"I just think Bobby Bose makes sense, Gray. He's the only one who's ever threatened your dad in any way."

"That we know of. I mean, there could be dozens of others with dozens of different motives. My father was married to one of the richest and most powerful women on the East Coast. Where there's money and power, there's trouble."

Stevie shrugs. He comes from money. A different kind of money (his father owns signage rights for nearly the entire world's fleet of commercial aircraft) but money nonetheless, and no one has been murdered in his family, so I guess I understand from whence this shrug comes.

"Dinner?"

"No," I tell him. "I'm beat. But I owe you. For flying us over today, I owe you dinner out."

"My choice?"

"Sure. Where would you like to go?"

"Phoenix."

"Very funny."

"I'm serious," Stevie says. "Phoenix. Haven't seen my parents in months. That's where I want you to take me."

I think about all the vacation time I've used up. I think of all the personal days I've taken in my quest to find Father's exterminator. It's not like it matters if I get fired. I always have the cushion. A rather large cushion, to be frank. An entire sofa, actually. But I've always kept my parents' wealth at arm's length. Except for the Gloucester Street penthouse. But that's another story. Which I've already told you.

"Fine, Stevie. Phoenix it is. We'll set a date. You call and make reservations."

"We don't need to book a flight," he argues. "I'll fly us."

From the driver's seat I glare at his profile until he senses my silent indignation and turns to look at me, and then I promptly say, "If you think for one minute I'm going to let you fly me out to Phoenix in your Chitty Chitty Bang Bang of a plane, then I retract my offer."

"*Luftpussy* is fine."

"You take that *Luftpussy* to the luftgynecologist or I'm never boarding your flying cunt again."

He feigns disgust. "How dare you speak that way!"

"Book a flight," I tell him. "And make reservations for us at the Biltmore."

"The Phoenician."

"The Biltmore."

"We'll stay at my parents' house."

"Good night."

☽

There are three messages on my machine. One is from Chaka telling me she doesn't appreciate my Sperm of the Year comment to Kamal Kareem. She thinks it was childish. Fuck her. I think getting collagen injections to make your lips look more African-American is childish. But I don't bring it up.

Not to her. Did I mention the liposuction transplant she had done in Los Angeles? I kid not. Chaka would kill me if she knew I went public with this, but the horrifying truth is a doctor in Beverly Hills took the fat he sucked out of an aging starlet's thighs and pumped it all into my sister's behind so she could, well, enjoy the same padding in the posterior that is enjoyed by many of her her black sisters. Kamal Kareem loves her new ass. And according to Chaka, so does his family.

The other message is from Ben. "Just called to say hi!" He never calls to say hi. He never calls from an out-of-town business trip. Come to think of it, he never calls. He wants to suck my dick.

I'm sure of it.

Lo and behold, the third message is from Pedro.

"I'm coming home tomorrow night," he says happily. He recites his flight number and arrival time into the machine and then says, "Can't wait to see you, Gray."

Looks like I'll be back at Logan Airport in twenty-four hours...

☽

The constellations must be masturbating. You know, shooting stars...and the milky way. I stare up into the sky and see how clear it is up there, and under a shower of starlight I have to believe this is one of those times in my life when anything can happen.

Sure enough, something does. Something big.

Life, it seems, is jerking me off.

I enter Terminal B. I check the arrivals screen; Flight 1540 from San Juan, Puerto Rico, is on time.

That's good. But I still have a moment for a coffee. So I stop into Starbucks and ask for a cup of the day's special: Colombian Cartel. Well, I don't remember exactly what it was called, but it sounded more like smuggled drugs and contraband than anything remotely resembling Maxwell House.

I return to the gate area and find that the arrivals screen has changed. Flight 1540 from San Juan, Puerto Rico, is no longer on time.

Maybe Pedro has changed his mind, I fear. I don't think he's capable of hijacking the plane back home, but having been gone for so long, he's like a stranger to me now. Little do I know how strange.

"The plane is in the area," the gate agent tells me. "But it's in a holding pattern."

"Any explanation?"

She smiles a very fake smile, one that actually says *fuck you* through the narrow line between her teeth (reddened by lipstick). "I'm afraid not. Could be just heavy traffic. Fog. Who knows?"

"Funny, I thought maybe you would."

She tilts her head. "Maybe the in-flight movie didn't finish in time," she says with a *chuckle-chuckle tee-hee.*

I am so not amused. I cut to the chase. "Did they crash?"

She is horrified. I guess saying "crash" at an airport goes over about as well as saying "80 proof" at an AA meeting. "Of course not!" she cries. "When I have more information I'll pass it on to those of you waiting. Now, if you'll excuse me..." She turns away from me and vacates her podium.

An hour passes, and I'm feeling airport-clammy. And I don't know about the sky, but my eyes are certainly fogged in. I'm seeing hazy now. I consider another cup of Medellín Mambo but then think otherwise. Where the hell is Flight 1540?

The gate agent returns.

"The aircraft is still circling," she says.

"They're going to run out of fuel!" I warn her, as if she might suddenly strap on her own set of wings and bring them a gallon.

"Unlikely," she tells me with a patronizing grin.

"*Un*likely? You're not supposed to say *un*likely. You're

supposed to say impossible, absolutely impossible, they have enough fuel to fly back to San Juan."

She ignores me flawlessly.

Ten minutes later (a total now of an hour and twenty-five minutes of unrelenting worry, which I get, incidentally, from my neurotic Jewish genes), the agent reaches for her handset and addresses those of us waiting in the gate area. It all seems so very routine.

"We are pleased to announce the arrival of Flight 1540 from San Juan, Puerto Rico. Passengers will be deplaning in just a few moments."

I wait for the faces. I see the faces. The first-class types get off first. They are well-tanned and already stressing out about returning to work. Some carry tennis racquets. Others carry martinis. Then comes coach. Sunburned and exhausted. Kids make noise. Parents, at the end of their one huge collective rope, shush them impatiently.

More faces. More noise. I hear happy greetings, slaps on the back (men-who-don't-kiss greeting men-who-don't-kiss), lots of laughter. And then I see Pedro. He smiles when our eyes meet. But then his eyes dart away. He looks like he's trying to adjust over his shoulder a luggage strap that needs no adjusting.

He looks nervous.

Of course he's nervous. He comes walking off the plane into my arms and says, "I'm going to be a woman."

I shake my head and say "What? What are you talking about?"

And he says, "I'm going to be a woman," and he's not even whispering and you can hear his voice above the whole crowd of people in the concourse, so I pull him to the side and we stand there huddling by one of the big windows that looks out to the purple night and the planes are sitting there soaked in heavy floodlight, shining like they were just painted for the first time, and I look right at him and I say, "What did they do to you in Puerto Rico?"

He just smiles and shrugs, and then he laughs.

"Stop it, Pedro," I beg him. "I don't want you to have a vagina. What am I supposed to do with a vagina?" I ask, thinking this is a silly game. A joke he planned on his tedious flight home. "I like you and your penis just the way they are. This changes everything."

Then we're in the car. The smell of Jane Seymour fills the air.

"Look," he says, his hands turned upward holding the air like a priest at Mass, "I met these women in Puerto Rico, you know. They had this operation, and I got to do what I got to do."

He is serious. I shiver. I can't catch my breath.

"Are we still a couple, Pedro?"

He says nothing.

"But I don't want a girlfriend. I want a boyfriend."

"But you love *me,* right? You love me, not what's dangling like a *chorizo* between my legs."

"No, no, no. I love you and all of you, and that includes the *chorizo* dangling between your legs. It's all part of the package."

Then I roll my eyes and on their way up into my head they fix on the sky and that's when I see how clear the sky is and how all the stars are floating around like come spurting from the Big Dipper.

So I look back at Pedro and see the same boyfriend I saw weeks ago when I dropped his sorry Puerto Rican ass at the airport. His dark, smooth skin, his mischievous brown eyes, his small nose carved into his face, which always reminds me of the sculptures I saw when he and I decided we were starved for culture and dragged ourselves out of bed one rainy afternoon at three o'clock and hailed a taxi to the museum. You know, I saw the head of Jesus, with the Mother Mary, or somebody, and I said, "Jesus, he's got your nose, Pedro." And here I am now, looking at the same Pedro and the same nose, the same goddamn person, and yet I am blown away, like completely Space Shuttle Challengered into fucking oblivion. He doesn't say much, riding here in the car beside me, his precious, tender meat tucked tightly into the folds of his jeans, and I stare at him, wondering what the hell has happened; this sex-change thing came completely out of nowhere. Oh, that crotch! Who knew how precious, how fleeting it really was? No wonder he sounded so cryptic over the telephone. No wonder his mother sounded just fine; there was no family crisis. There was a Pedro crisis. A battle between the penis that was and the vagina that could be.

I'm getting woozy.

"Obviously you went to too many drag shows in San Juan," I say.

Then he puts his hands on my knees.

I want to smack him.

But I love his lips. They are so thick without being stupid-looking or abnormal and they could suck your face, and everything else, right in, and kiss velvet kisses all over you. I don't want him to bleed.

"Huh? Too many drag shows," I insist.

"Fuck you."

"No, fuck you."

"You'll be able to do just that when I'm a girl."

All of a sudden I start to cry. I feel the weight of the tears against the bottom lids of my eyes, and my cheeks start to rise and then I just let go.

"You're crying," Pedro says.

"No shit, Sherlock-in-a-dress."

Pedro laughs.

So do I. I love him so much. "Why can't you have a penis *and* a vagina? I think I could deal with that."

"We'll see."

I hate when people say "We'll see." My mother would always say "We'll see" when I wanted something that she wasn't ready to give me, like a new bike or a hockey stick or sometimes even an ice cream cone at the end of a hot summer day.

"We'll sleep on it," he says. "We'll sleep on it."

"Have you really given this a lot of thought?"

"Really."

"Really?"

"Look, Gray, I'm a classic case. A woman stuck in a man's body."

I shake my head as I spin the steering wheel and turn the car into our garage. "No, Pedro, you are a classic case of a man stuck in an asshole's body."

"That would make me straight. And I'm definitely not straight."

"Truth is, after six years, I don't know who you are."

"Don't start that."

☽

Pedro is unpacking his bags now, throwing curled-up, rumpled balls of dirty underwear into piles on the floor; I can't look anymore. I just can't look. I used to react to that underwear like a canine beast, sniffing out some secret treasure, panting and drooling until I dug it up and brought it home.

He looks at me.

I look away.

"Sleep on it, Gray," he reminds me.

He gets in on his side and I get in on my side. I stare at the ceiling and say my prayers.

I talk to God and ask for my father, and I think God says "We'll see" but then Father touches me with his hand and I smile. His presence lingers too briefly then leaves.

Pedro is already snoring.

I wake him up and we fuck.

I watch him spill his big dipper and I think, *This may be the last time.* "Oh, Gray, this is heaven!" he cries.

"No, this is orgasm," I correct him.

"Everyone deserves a chance at both."

He rolls over and falls asleep, his chest rising and falling with his breath and his dreams and everything else he is keeping to himself.

☽

Man, oh, man.

I wake up as anxious as a meteor plummeting to Earth. I dash to the window and face the pristine sky.

Things are different now.

Fifteen

I remember now my dreams from last night. Vaginas, what else? I dreamed of huge, gaping vaginas. Vagina monsters, thugs, hoodlums, if you will, blocking the way to my front door. (Gee, what could that mean?). One vagina was particularly rude; she (he, it?) spat at me and told me to fuck off. What could I say? Except, "I thought you just did."

My only protection: a can of FDS feminine hygiene spray. One can in each hand, I challenged the vagina to a duel. *Psst. Psst. Psst.*

Thank God Pedro exhaled one of his infamous stench clouds from his anus or I might not have woken up from the dream uninjured, unswallowed, unheterosexualized by the Fighting Vaginas. (And understand this: I mean no disrespect to real woman and real vaginas. Long may they reign. Let them rule the world. Let them become the penis of the next century. But please do not give one to Pedro.)

"Pedro," I say later when we are standing beside each other in the kitchen, preparing our respective breakfasts (toast, cereal, and a chocolate chip cookie for me; blueberries, cottage cheese, and Midol for him), "we need to talk."

He groans and puts a hand to his head, indicating an ache deep inside his skull. "No, Gray. Just leave it alone."

"Leave it alone?"

"Let it go."

"Sorry, Pedro, you don't just come home and announce

you're switching sexes and expect me to *let it go*?"

"No," he tells me, "I expect you to give it a chance."

"What kind of chance?" I ask him as I make my way to the dining table.

"Be patient. We'll see if you can adjust."

I look out the tremendous windows at an otherwise quiet morning and the indifferent river below. I do see a chill in the air—maybe it's the current on the Charles, racing in V's, or maybe it's the color of leaves clinging to the ancient trees along the esplanade. I don't know. "I doubt it," I tell my husband/wife.

"I'm performing at Damsels."

My eyes leap from the view and soar into Pedro's face. "You're what? You're performing in drag now? Is there anything else you haven't told me?"

"What do you think I was doing in Puerto Rico?"

"Getting an operation."

He smiles devilishly. He's sitting opposite me, his back to the window. I wonder if pushing him out is an option. "I think I proved last night that there's been no operation yet."

I say nothing and take a bite of toast. It crunches like a crouton and I imagine that everywhere we go now, Pedro will order salads to keep his girlish figure.

"I'm doing drag, Gray, to test the waters."

"What waters?"

"What it's like to be a woman."

I *tsk* a disgusted *tsk*. "There's a difference between being a transvestite and being a transsexual, you know. You don't have to do drag to get a sex change!"

Pedro's hand freezes in front of his mouth. A berry dangles. "I *know* that," he tells me. "But I thought it was a rather clever idea. You know, a dress rehearsal for my new life... Get it, a *dress* rehearsal?"

"I get it."

"And Damsels is supposed to be the best drag stage in

the world. Even my friends from Paris say so."

"You have friends from Paris?"

"A few...Michel, Fabrice, Tristan, and Helga."

"Helga?" I ask, amused, while my cereal gets soggy.

"She's my trainer. She's staging the show at Damsels with all her French beauties."

"So where do you fit into the picture?"

"They needed someone to be Charo. So they were looking for a Hispanic like me."

"Charo?"

"Yes, you know, *cootchie cootchie...*"

"I'm going to be sick," I say, rising from the table. My shoulders shudder. My eyes are about to unleash yet another bucket of tears.

"Honey, you'll come, won't you? You'll come to see the show?"

"Yes. I'll bring my own tampon."

He throws a berry at me. Then another. "You are such an asshole!"

"Fuck it while you can."

He slams his fist on the table. It rattles. I turn around. He sees the hurt in my eyes, the first signs of weeping. His face softens, acquiesces.

"Gray, I'm sorry. I know this is hard for you. But please, I need your support. I'm counting on it."

We stare at each other in this silence, like two hockey players at a puckless face-off. I don't know what to do with this moment as it lingers and breathes in and out and becomes its own creature between us.

The tears are inching slowly toward my chin. Within seconds they will fall to the floor and dissolve into the history of this magnificent place. Unless someone walks across the room before they dry; then they'll just be beads of a watery footprint.

"Okay. I'll be there. When is it?"

"Two Saturdays from now."

"Fine," I say, dumping the mush of bran and raisin down the disposal, "but I'm taking off to Phoenix first."

I am prepared for takeoff. Now more than ever.

Sixteen

Pedro goes to work.

So do I.

Ben is still out of town. I want so badly to riffle through his desk and see if he stashes pornography there. Male pornography. Huge dicks and massive chests. I'm very tempted but surprised by my own better judgment. Of what do I need proof? The airport kiss—or rather, *mouth-jacking*—is proof enough that this man is a mixed-up, confused hetero-homo in search of a safe place to plant his sex and sexuality.

Work is better than usual. Only in the sense that things are more relaxed when Ben isn't around. The women in the secretary pool are chatty, less catty; there's more laughter. I'm wearing jeans. In the middle of the day I get an erection and I don't know why. Perhaps because I have this fantasy of Ben charging in here, stripping me naked, and taking me on the desk. I'm still entering data into my computer as he's entering me. I realize this is so inappropriate (not sex during data entry, but sex with my boss), and I know I'll never get involved with a mixed-up, confused hetero-homo in search of a safe place to plant his sex and sexuality. I know this urge between my legs is a function of the alienation I feel from Pedro. If he won't need me, love me, who will? Then again, I must admit this Ben thing started before I had any idea of Pedro's crazy plan.

I take a long lunch.

I've tried calling Stevie all morning to see if he can join me, but he's not around. I keep getting his machine. I could really use my best friend in the world right about now. He'd listen to my problems. He'd figure it all out. He'd draw a picture of Pedro in a dress and we'd probably laugh.

But my best friend in the world can't draw.

He's dead.

I choke on my Mile-High (6 inches) Turkey Club and gasp for breath.

No one notices.

I've just seen the midday newscast. Ben's wife is filling in for the noon anchor who's "on assignment" (probably a bad hair day), and her top story is the crash of a private plane in the waters off Logan Airport. It happened last night. Planes were forced to circle (Pedro's among them, I now realize) while rescue crews tried to locate the wreckage. Their efforts failed. It wasn't until ten o'clock this morning that crews reached the downed aircraft. A twin-engine Cessna Titan. I watch the video closely. The tail section juts from the water like the fin of a shark. Waves lap about the fuselage. As crews twist the plane's carcass, the tail numbers are revealed: N-7404.

N-7404, engraved now in the sea like a birth date on a headstone. N-7404. I know it well. Stevie's plane. My eyes don't believe my eyes, so they close against the horror of the truth. But still, a certain memory slips through this blindness, not unlike the gathering of light that wakes me each morning.

"N-7404 requests permission to taxi."

"N-7404 on final approach."

"N-7404 to field, one passenger."

I want to scream.

I need help.

Crews are still looking for bodies. None have been recovered. It's believed the pilot was the only occupant of the aircraft. (Is Marla smiling?)

I panic.

Blood rushes from my head.

(Is Marla shimmying her shoulders?)

Help me.

The choking continues.

(And heaving her breasts?)

It's Stevie's plane.

He's dead.

I begged him to have *Luftpussy* checked before he flew again. I begged him! All that banging. Something was terribly wrong.

Am I going to puke?

Suddenly someone notices my distress. It's a waitress. Her name is Connie, or Lonnie, or Donnie. I can't really read her name tag amid the convulsions. Somehow she stands me up, bends me over, locks her arms below my rib cage, and jolts upward.

As though this had been rehearsed, as though I had actually studied my part, bits and pieces of masticated turkey, lettuce (no tomato), and bacon eject from my mouth in a sudden spray, and the waitress says, "Well done."

I look at her. Her name is Bonnie. "You saved my life," I tell her.

"Are you okay?"

"My best friend in the world just died."

She looks at me sadly, sympathetically. Then I see confusion wrinkle across her forehead. "And you came *here* for lunch?"

"I just found out," I whimper, pointing to the TV. "I just saw it on the news."

I tell her about the plane crash. About Stevie. How I have to carry his casket. She doesn't understand. I try to explain, but impatient hungry eyes glare at her and she has orders to take.

I'm surrounded by images of Stevie's body floating, maybe devoured by big beasts of the ocean. Maybe I'll never see him again. Maybe I'll never even get a chance to peek into the casket when no one is looking. I see images also of *Luftpussy* all tangled up in the sea. I'm sobbing as I leave the restaurant and call Chaka for help from the cell phone Stevie gave me for my birthday a few years ago.

He had sent a man in a G-string to my door. The man was holding a silver platter. The man was gorgeous. On the platter rested the cell phone. The man said his name was Dick. I believed him. The phone was ringing. I lifted it from the silver platter and said, "Hello?" "Happy birthday," Stevie replied.

I hope Stevie knew that a) I never fucked Dick; and b) his friendship was the greatest gift I'll ever receive.

Seventeen

Chaka is waiting for me at the penthouse when I arrive.

She throws her arms around me and joins me in tears. She says she's sorry a dozen times; I wish she'd stop. When people say they're sorry about the death of a loved one I just want to scream, "What are you sorry for? It's not your fault!" At Father's funeral, though, I allowed people to say they were sorry, because after all, I suspected anyone and everyone of his murder, and any one of those apologies could have actually meant, "I'm sorry. I did it. I killed your Pop."

"I told him to have the damn plane checked!" I cry.

"I know you did."

"I'm having a rough time with vaginas these days. First *Luftpussy* crashes, then Pedro tells me he wants one."

Instinctively, it seems, Chaka crosses her legs. "A plane?" she asks.

"A pussy."

I explain Pedro's plan. She couldn't be more stunned had Kamal Kareem told her he was leaving her for a white woman. She doesn't know what to say. But she shakes her head convincingly. She feels bad. Real bad. Then she freezes. Her mouth unhinges and opens wider than wide. "We need to go see Brenda."

"What?"

"Now," she says. "We go now and maybe you can catch Stevie before he fully crosses to the other side."

"You're an idiot," I tell my sister. "He died last night. He's already crossed. Checked in. Been to the cocktail party."

"Who are we to say how long the journey takes? I'm telling you, Brenda's work will be easier. Stevie is still hovering. He must be. She won't have to place such a long-distance call."

"Long-distance call?"

"To heaven. Figuratively speaking."

I ponder.

"You want to speak to him, don't you?"

"Of course."

"Then it's settled," Chaka says happily. She rewraps her hair and leads me to the door.

She insists we fly. I balk. I call it tragic irony. She calls it fast and efficient and reminds me how bone-chilling cold a ferry crossing in the fall can be. We board Provincetown/Boston Airways Flight 777 for Martha's Vineyard Airport. I feel like a traitor. I look out the egg-shaped window and stare at the puny view. I choose one ripple among the millions wrinkling the vast blue blanket of ocean below; that ripple is my farewell kiss to Stevie Goldman.

☽

Brenda meets us outside *Entre Tetas*.

There is no Yugo.

"Where's Derderva?" I ask.

"I've given him some research to do into Bobby Bose. In the event your grandmother is wrong, Derderva may have the answer with that manifest."

Chaka sighs. "Really, I'm quite sure my ex-husband had nothing to do with this. If he were here last summer, someone would have noticed. He's so *not* Martha's Vineyard."

Brenda chuckles. Her several chins absorb the shock.

"Shall we begin?" she asks, looking wistfully at our front door.

I shrug. Chaka nods eagerly. We enter. We file to our usual spot in the usual room. Lourdes purrs to the left, purrs to the right (though I do believe Brenda has the route mapped out in her head by now). We sit. Hold hands. Brenda is heaving out a deep breath when I ask, "Could it be too early to do this? Do we risk interrupting his trip to the other side?"

Brenda ignores me, save for the snarl that uncurls across her face.

"Gray, I told you, the timing is perfect," Chaka insists.

"She's right," Brenda says quietly. "We'll catch him on his way."

On his way?

I watch her intently as she turns wholly to her work, as she sinks to new levels of concentration (new to me). Brenda whispers. Her lips barely move. The room is lighter than usual. We have lit the candles, but they're upstaged by the late-afternoon sun on its autumn mission through our palatial windows. Prisms in the sunlight stream in like a storm of rainbows. Oh, how it feels like it is raining true irony; I am drenched in sadness and promise. Beauty and despair. I am struck now by soft bullets, maybe raindrops, that I absorb into my skin at the magnificence of this loss. I shed tears, here. No one seems to notice. My face is soaked. Then my grief turns to worry. Have Stevie's parents been notified? Should I call them? If they haven't been told, do I want to be the one to deliver the news? Over the phone? Maybe I should fly to Phoenix today.

"Whatever it is," Brenda says in my direction, "Stevie will tell you what to do."

I'm rattled. "How did you know what I was thinking?"

"I didn't," Brenda replies, "but I knew you'd have questions."

Our hands tighten around one another's.

"Of course I have questions. I want to know what happened. That's perfectly natural, don't you think? I mean, the guy is, was, still is, always will be, my best friend..."

Brenda smiles. "Then shut up, Gray, and let me go get him."

Shut up? Well, that was unnecessary and rather unbecoming of a medium. But I let it slide. Brenda scares me.

We wait. For contact. That's what Brenda calls it sometimes: contact. My mind wanders (what else is new?). I'm not concentrating because I'm thinking of what it will be like to have Stevie on my shoulder, his resting place resting on me. I will carry the casket as promised. I won't let go until it sinks into the ground. I will say my own prayers. I will learn to fly. I'm terrified of the thought of sitting behind the controls, of manning my own ship, but someone needs to make sure the legacy of Stevie Goldman lives on. But I will not name my plane *Luftpussy II*. I just can't. Stevie would understand. He knows that as much as I appreciate the idea of vagina (after all, it was my port of entry into this world), I have no business trying to emulate his fascination for them. I don't know what I'll name my plane. First I must see if I can get off the ground.

The table wiggles.

Here he comes.

Brenda takes her hands from ours and holds them flat against the air above her. The table continues to wiggle. And then it spins. I'm getting whacked in the knee by one of its legs, once per revolution.

"I'm here," says a voice cascading down the walls. "You can have a few minutes of my time."

A chill begins to rush my spine but stops halfway up.

It's not Stevie. It's not his voice. It's a woman's voice.

"Hello Graydove, Norma Lee, Brenda, Lourdes..."

"Grandma?" I ask.

"Yes, sweetheart. It's me again."

I look at Brenda. She senses my glare and shrugs.

"No offense, Grandma, but we were looking for Stevie," Chaka tells her.

"Yes, Grandma, do you bring news about Stevie?"

"Stevie? Who's Stevie?"

"You know Stevie. My best friend."

"Oh, Stevie Goldman, of course. I'm sorry, children, he isn't here."

"But we don't expect he's made it all the way to the other side yet, Grandma," I explain.

"What other side?"

"You know...the other side...where you are."

"We don't call it 'the other side.' We call it 'Valley of Happy Clouds.' "

"Sounds like a rest home."

"It's a Native American thing," Grandmother says. "You wouldn't understand."

"Stevie was killed in a plane crash yesterday," I explain. "I don't suppose he's made it all the way up there yet. We're hoping to catch him on the way."

Clearly Brenda has relinquished control of this séance—either fed up with Chaka and me or convinced we can handle this on our own—and she's just sitting across from us stroking her pussy, Lourdes.

Meanwhile, Grandmother has started humming a tune I don't recognize. It's not one of her fabled lullabies. More like a show tune. A love ballad. "He's not here, Gray. But wait a minute—I'll go check today's manifest to see if he's expected. Be right back!"

Brenda folds her hands in front of her. Lourdes meows indignantly as the petting ends. "To do this successfully," the medium tells us, "you two must steer the communication more precisely."

"What does that mean?" I ask.

"You're all over the place. Stick to the task at hand. Like I've always said, think of it as a long-distance call. You're running up the bill."

I give her a saucy grin that she can't see, but I replicate the sauciness in my voice when I say, "We're very rich. We don't worry about bills. Are you trying to tell us our *meter* has expired?"

Nobody laughs.

"Besides," I add, "I thought you agreed this one was free."

"I did. But that doesn't mean I have to sit quietly while you develop all these bad habits."

Sometimes I'm not sure about Brenda Cloudholder. At times I love her like an old fat aunt; other times she reminds me of my high school drama club friend, Monica (also fat), who was a genuine fag hag in the making and made gay boys like me feel superior one moment and, lest we get too much attention and glamour and steal the spotlight, inferior the next.

Suddenly, the music of Sylvester: "Do You Want to Funk With Me?"

Our heads turn. Our eyes zip across the room. Grandmother is back.

"Grandma? When did you learn *that* song?"

A celestial laugh fills the room. "Oh, children, it is such a gas here in the Valley of Happy Clouds."

"A gas?"

"Well, yes, my darlings. You don't think we spend all our time floating around up here watching over *you,* do you?"

"I guess I was kind of hoping..."

"Sorry, Gray. They call it heaven for a reason. Anything goes."

"Even outdated disco?"

"God loves disco, Gray. It's a fact."

"That's just fine, ma'am," Brenda interjects, "but do tell us of the boy...Stevie Goldman. Any word on him?"

"I'm afraid not," she says. "Water landings are complicated."

A knock on the door.

"Water landings?" Brenda asks.

"We like them dry when they arrive," she says. "Wet souls cause too much distress down below. Heavy rains. Flash floods. What do you think caused the great floods of the Midwest a few years back?"

"Rivers overflowing?" I suggest.

Another knock at the door.

"Can we answer it in the middle of a séance?" Chaka asks the medium.

Brenda shrugs. "Might as well, with the direction this one is going." She sounds frazzled, in an ethereal sort of way. Like static electricity is zapping through her fairy dust.

"Oh, absolutely, answer the door," Grandma urges. "I have all the time in the world."

As I rise from the table and head for the front door I hear my grandmother above, sweetly humming "It's Raining Men," and I shake my head, unable to conjugate the verbs of heaven. I wonder how long it took Jessica Savitch to get there. Probably a very long time.

I call "Wait a minute" to the visitor. Moments later I swing open the imposing door. But no one is there.

"Hul—lo?"

And then, from beyond the door frame steps a figure, a bag slung over his shoulder, a huge, familiar smile slung from ear to ear.

It's Stevie Goldman.

I pass out.

Eighteen

At least I think I'm passing out.

I see fuzz, then black, then I whack my head.

On the floor? I'm not sure. Next thing I know I'm stretched out on the drawing room divan, slapped on the face, splashed with water. That scent of Lagerfeld.

My eyes open. There he his. Still smiling. Chaka has him in a headlock. She's crying uncontrollably. If she doesn't let go, I fear he will certainly die this time.

"You're not dead," I say.

"Shut up!" he replies, coming forward, Chaka still around his neck.

"No! No! He's alive! He's alive!" my sister cries.

"Yes, he's alive," Stevie says, "and rather put out that you'd have a séance without him, thank you very much."

"Well, that *is* rather mortal of you to cop an attitude," I tell him. "Very mortal, and fabulously gay."

He laughs.

I laugh.

Everyone laughs.

Then I cry. I sob. I whimper and simper and *waaah, waah, waaah* all over the place. "I thought you were dead," I tell him.

Chaka releases him. Stevie slides onto the divan by my side and lies across my chest. "Of course I'm not dead."

"But what about *Luftpussy*?"

"It was my mechanic, Earl." Stevie's smile is gone. He lifts himself from me, and his deep, thoughtful stare invades me like a lover. I absorb, completely wipe up, sponge the pain in his eyes. "It could have been me. It should have been me. It could have been *us*. We made it back to Boston. And just as I promised I had the plane checked out. Earl was on a test flight when it crashed into the ocean."

I inhale sharply. "Oh, my God, Stevie. Oh, no."

"The hard part was telling his family. All twelve of them."

"Tell me about it...I was going to have to tell yours."

"I'm so sorry to have worried you like that," Stevie says.

"Well, when I heard the news, and I couldn't get a hold of you, I feared the worst, I figured the worst. I assumed the worst. It was devastating."

"Oh, Graydove. What can I say? I'll never die on you again. Promise." Stevie sits completely upright now, and his posture is as serious as his eyes. "Something happened here," he says. "Something happened to my plane here, and I'm going to find out what it was. We had trouble, probably engine trouble, on the way back home the other night. And then the plane doesn't survive a routine safety check." He shakes his head. "I hate to say this, but someone working maintenance on my plane here might have really fucked up. The past forty-eight hours have been the worst nightmare you can imagine."

Brenda Cloudholder appears from the shadows of the séance room. "I've sent your grandmother back and have disconnected for the day."

"Your grandmother?" Stevie asks.

"We were having a séance. For you."

Tears fill his eyes. "You're kidding. I was wondering what you were doing here."

"We needed to talk to you," I say.

A drop rolls down his cheek. "I was driving by, and I saw your rental out in the driveway. I couldn't imagine you'd come to the island without telling me."

"No. The plan was to communicate with you the only way we know how to communicate with...the dead."

"I'm not dead," he says, embracing me again. My neck is wet from his tears. "I'm not dead," he repeats. "Tell me you believe me."

I hold him away for a second. "Part of me believes you."

"Part of you?"

"Part of me fears I'll wake up from this fainting spell and find that you still haven't been heard from."

"You have woken from the fainting spell," Chaka assures me. "And we're all here. All the people that matter. Auntie Em and Toto too."

☽

Derderva comes for Brenda. He has no news about Bobby Bose. And no personality, still, to speak of.

Chaka, Stevie, and I agree to spend the night at *Entre Tetas*.

Stevie and I share a room, and before we drift off to sleep we attempt a verbal investigation of *Luftpussy*'s demise.

"The mechanics here are not the best and the brightest, if you know what I mean," Stevie says. He's wrapped up in a velvet blanket, lying peacefully on the bed opposite mine. I smell his presence now. That Stevie smell. That subtle aroma of a heterosexual friend whom I love but am not in love with. He is the brother I never had. Yes, Kirkland exists, but still I insist, Stevie is the brother I never had. I want to build a fort with him. I want to tie our sheets to the bedposts and unearth a special passageway and crawl underneath this tented hideaway.

"You think one of them fucked up your plane?"

"The thing is, there was nothing wrong with my plane. I never requested any maintenance."

"You think they did work on your plane they were supposed to do on someone else's?"

"Sounds rather implausible, don't you think?"

I sit up and shrug. "I don't know. You tell me they're not the best and the brightest. So maybe it's possible."

"I did a preflight inspection."

"Yes, we watched."

"I did everything I was supposed to do. Nothing showed up irregular."

"Now you're blaming yourself?"

"A man is dead, Graydove. He died on my plane. It's only by some whack of fate that it wasn't us."

"Twist."

"What?"

"Of fate. Twist, not whack."

"Whack this..."

"That would be incest," I say.

Stevie smiles. He knows it's true. "You know, Gray, you're lucky to be alive. For some reason the real malfunction waited till we were safe at home and claimed somebody else's life. An innocent man's life."

"I'm an innocent man."

"Yes, and you're alive."

"This isn't your fault."

"Maybe it was sabotage." His voice is beginning to drift.

"Sabotage?"

"Jesse Helms was here last week."

"You think Jesse Helms sabotaged your plane?"

He laughs a sleepy laugh. I doubt, for a moment, that there will be an answer, sensing that his responses are in a thunder and lightning sort of way, coming at longer and longer intervals from the questions. But I am wrong. "No, I don't think *he* sabotaged anything," Stevie says. "But someone might have wanted to do something funky to *his* plane and hit mine by mistake."

"On the Vineyard?"

"Sure. Why not? Helms is hated everywhere."

"True. But Vineyard people don't sabotage. They write letters to the editor and exclude you from parties."

"Look, Gray, all I'm saying is it's very odd how Jesse Helms flies into town on a similar plane, and then mine goes down only days later."

"How do you know he flies the same kind of plane?"

No answer.

"Stevie?"

He shudders awake. "What?"

"How do you know you and Helms fly the same plane?"

"Minerva told me."

"Minerva?"

"You know, Brenda's little helper."

I shake my head and lie down again. "Derderva."

"Yeah, him."

"How does he know?"

"He knows, Gray. He knows. He's been poking around the airport for days checking out the Bobby Bose theory, trying to see if Bobby flew into Martha's Vineyard airport, you know, around the time of your dad's...murd— death."

"It's okay, Stevie. You can say 'murder.' "

"Murder."

"Well, at least Derderva has been helpful in some way. So far he's turned up nothing else."

"We still on for Phoenix this weekend?" Stevie asks.

"I don't see why not."

"We'll fly commercial."

"I was planning on it."

"Oh, really? Now you don't trust me to fly. That's what I was afraid of." He flounces into another position. The bed creaks angrily.

"No," I correct him in an even voice. "I want to fly first-class."

"Who's paying?"

"I am," I tell him. "For both of us. Now go to sleep."

He has gone already.

"I love you," I say.

There is, of course, no answer. But I know he loves me too.

❩

I am making love to David (Michelangelo's David), and Barry White ("Can't Get Enough of Your Love, Baby") is providing the score. Live. But he's not looking. The Italian police burst through the door and ask me for my passport, visa, license, and registration. License and registration? But I'm not driving, I frantically explain. Just kidding, they tell me. You Americans are all so serious. They want to know if I have a permit to fuck a major work of art. I reach for my pocket, then realize there is no pocket to reach for because I'm naked.

That's when the music wakes me up. A moment so promising, yet so stark and vulnerable is interrupted. Probably for the better.

At first I was afraid, I was petrified...
Thinking I could never live without you as my bride...
But then I spent so many nights thinking how you did me wrong...
I grew strong.
I learned how to wear a thong.

"What the fuck?" comes from Stevie, whose naked torso emerges from the heap of velvet.

I shake myself more awake and give a shrug of all shrugs. "How the hell do I know?"

We both start like we're going to move and investigate the source of this music, but then we exchange eerie glances and scare ourselves frozen.

Suddenly Chaka bounds through the door to our room, her hair the logo of insanity. We gasp. We flinch. She begs us come. She has more balls than the two of us combined. She was stirred from sleep by the music too and insists on checking it out. But not alone.

We go. Chaka as bodyguard. Her hair, if nothing else, looks dangerous. We round a few corners, creep down the wide, three-story main staircase, and follow the music. The song is coming from (where else?) our room of many séances.

We enter. Slowly.

"I guess Brenda did not exactly disconnect," Chaka whispers.

"Huh?" Stevie whispers.

"From the other side..." Chaka explains. "One of her ghosts has lingered."

Oh, no, now go...
Walk out the door.
But leave your pumps here
The ones Imelda always wore...
Aren't you the one who tried to cut me from the will...
I'd love you still,
Without your hundred mill...

And so the three of us stare at the ceiling with the bewildered resignation of any three adults who realize that ghosts will be ghosts.

Only one thing bothers me.

I wonder if it bothers Chaka or Stevie.

I don't say anything, because I don't want to plant ideas in their heads or give them any reason to entertain mine. I trust they know Gloria Gaynor like I know Gloria Gaynor.

This is not Gloria Gaynor.

It was her the first time.

But now it sounds (albeit remotely) more like Father.

Nineteen

Jesse Helms is an asshole. And quite possibly a homosexual. Reverse the psychology. Figure it out. Anyone who hates homos that much must have a hard time looking in the mirror. If Jesse *is* a queer, he should drag his sorry, saggy ass and shriveled dinkie out of the closet. Then go back in. We don't want him on our team.

Why do I mention Jesse Helms?

I mention Jesse Helms because there have been rumors that the North Carolina Republican was on Martha's Vineyard, not simply for a vacation, it seems, but rather to look for a vacation rental. Brenda Cloudholder says she's heard (this is rumor, now, a few times removed) Helms had wanted to cut a deal to rent out *Entre Tetas* for his stay. But if you believe the stories, he suddenly changed his mind when he heard a homosexual (me) had once slept here and that the house displayed works subsidized by the NEA (funded by liberal Jewish homos), including a few pieces of "downright pornography!" (*Portrait of a Circumcision*), and that the place was haunted by lesbian ghosts (Juliet, though the lesbian thing was clearly invented).

Fuck you, Jesse. We wouldn't rent the house to you for all the tea in China (bad subject).

And that's where we left it when Stevie and I took off for Phoenix.

❩

"Pedro's not upset?" Stevie asks as we toss about in the airport-bound taxi.

"No. He's been rehearsing."

"Oh."

On the way back from the Vineyard a few days ago, I told Stevie all about Pedro's imminent sex change. He had been, of course, very understanding, and had told me he would support whatever I decided to do.

"Decided?"

"Whether or not to stay with him..."

"Stay with him? No fucking way. In fact, no fucking way if there's no way we'll be fucking. Get it?"

"I guess."

"I'm serious. He makes his choices. He lives with his choices. I do not have to learn to love something new between his legs."

☽

We're at the airport now. We're flying Western Airlines. It's the only airline with a nonstop flight between Boston and Phoenix. It's also the only airline where your shoes are considered legroom. That's the only reason we're flying first-class. Legroom. Ordinarily I don't give much thought to where I sit when I fly. Until someone can show me that first-class passengers walk away from airline disasters with their martinis still in hand and their luggage still intact, and first out on the carousel, I will stick to flying whatever's available. My brother, Kirkland, who needs no legroom because his legs are shorter than my thumbs, loves to fly first-class for a different reason. "I like being able to get on board first so I can stare down all the plebes who file past me into coach."

Kirkland is very serious about his superiority.

We are early. The flight is late.

"The delay should only be twenty minutes," Barbie (I kid you not) the gate agent tells us.

I have to pee.

Stevie stays with the carry-ons while I seek out the men's room. When I find it I discover that the urinals are occupied, so I slip into a stall and unzip. This peeing-in-public thing has always been a problem for me; I don't understand it, but somehow I just lose the urge.

I try to imagine waterfalls. Oceans. Faucets. But I am distracted.

The man sitting in the stall to my left explodes.

The man sitting in the stall to my right explodes.

Now I know how Switzerland felt during World War II.

At this decisively unattractive moment I zip back up, flush the empty toilet (lest someone should suspect me of poor rearing), and exit the men's room, my bladder full but my integrity intact.

We board last. No need to watch the "plebes file past."

There are four flight attendants assigned to the eight people in first-class. There are three assigned to the two hundred and three passengers in coach. Maybe I'll walk away from the crash with a martini and perhaps a new haircut. I'm not afraid of flying. I simply assume it's a fifty-fifty. Either we make it off the ground or we don't. Either we stay up there or we don't. Either we land safely or we don't. I do not realize I'm thinking this out loud and disturbing the other passengers around me, so it comes as somewhat of a surprise when Stevie tells me to shut the hell up.

I shut the hell up, and I fall asleep.

Bryan, the hunky, blue-eyed flight attendant with a bulge the size of Chicago, wakes me gently and asks me if I'd like to have dinner.

A date?

No, stupid, the meal service.

"The chicken or the beef?" he asks.

"I'll have your beef tonight."

He smiles.

So do I.

Stevie kicks me. Hard.

The meal is uneventful, save for the phone number slipped beneath my bread dish. Seems Bryan is laying over in Phoenix and would like some company. Man, oh, man, would I love to oblige. He is Kansas-cute, milk-fed like veal, oh-so-tender. And I realize suddenly I'm aging and turning into a pathetic old queen much too quickly. I'm still in my thirties. Why am I aching for youth? I'm still young. Am I not?

I am not.

According to gay chronology, I am close to retirement. Look but don't touch him. Unless you have a lot a money. If so, touch, but don't expect much in return. Certainly not love. Buy him a Porsche and all the best clothes, fly him to Cannes, and drench him in wine. But you're his sugar daddy, not his lover. I wouldn't be thinking this way, if not for Pedro. I wouldn't be feeling old and useless. I wouldn't be entertaining the idea of snuggling up to milk-fed veal in the middle of the desert if my man wasn't on the verge of becoming a woman.

Am I on the verge of a nervous breakdown?

I make a note to call Pedro Almodóvar and ask.

I politely nod at Bryan. I suppose I should feel okay and somewhat attractive that this young skystud would invite my interest. Then again, this is first-class. My wallet couldn't be too far behind.

☽

I fall asleep again and wake up in Phoenix.

There's a tendency to draw all sorts of poetic and stirring analogies to the phoenix, a mythical creature rising from its ashes, but it's late, my luggage is heavy, and I'm gassy.

Stevie's parents are waiting with arms outstretched for

both of us. They love me as if I'm one of their own, and in case I've forgotten that, they remind me.

Phoenix is really very beautiful.

The mountaintops, blacker than the night, scrape the sky in ways buildings cannot. It's as if the fingers of the earth are poking themselves through their molten gloves and reaching, always reaching for the stars that sit so contently up there in heaven.

We drive north and then east around Camelback. The town is called Paradise Valley. And every time I've been here it does feel very close to paradise, although there should be water. There are lush lagoons and waterfalls in paradise. I'm sure of it.

But the Goldmans have a spa. And it's a delightful treat after a five-hour flight, so I languish there without a care in the world and study the night as though the sky is geometry and the clouds a romance language. The soft desert breeze kisses my exposed skin. I see the silhouette of the Goldman family behind the glass windows that look out to this expansive backyard; they are full of laughter and loving gestures. I wish at this moment, and probably, I realize, only at this moment, that my family could be a lot more simple. A lot more *family* again. Sure, the Goldmans have money (they made a fortune designing those signs for airlines that remind you to PLEASE WIPE THE WASH BASIN AS A COURTESY TO THE NEXT PASSENGER, but they've never let it get ahead of them. It is money to them; that's all. In my family, the money has always been the driving force, the underlining tension, the fantasy and the reality, and everything and everyone (wanna-bes, hangers-on, gold diggers, extortionists) in between. My mother has always sworn it isn't so (as she slipped into a limo and out of the country). Still, we don't flaunt it; it's just there. The Goldmans don't flaunt it either, but it's different. I see how the money predicates their family, not the other way around.

They have a lovely desert home. Large and airy. High ceilings, windows galore. The house sits just below the camel's largest hump. Boulders, like muscles of the beast, protrude everywhere, hanging over the house itself. Dramatic but unnerving. No earthquakes here, they promise. Still, I can't help imagine what I might look like squashed at the bottom of a landslide. I think of Father and the blunt object that squashed his head.

Father.

I say a prayer for him in the stillness and beauty of this night.

I whisper "Father, Father, Father" into the canyon that surrounds me, into the majesty of how God left things.

Then I wrap a towel around my waist, adjust to the quick shiver of a desert chill, and find the guest room inside.

I'm in bed when Stevie pokes his head in and asks, "Are you comfortable?"

"Of course."

"Big day tomorrow," he says.

"Oh?"

"Shopping for a new plane."

"Is that why we're here?"

He smiles and shakes his head. "Of course not. I've been planning this trip for some time. The parents have been on my back for a visit."

"I'm glad we came. I like them. Always have."

"They like you too."

I tuck a pillow behind my head and lean up against the wall. "Maybe you'll return the favor?"

He sits on the edge of the bed and covers my knee with his hand. "How so, Gray?"

"Be with me when I visit my parents."

He tries not to show the wince behind the gracious smile he so artfully manages. "Sure...whatever you'd like, Gray."

"Only problem is this," I say. "One's in a jail, the other's in a cemetery."

"How about we bring flowers to them both?"

I smile. "You are too much."

"Good night, Gray."

"Good night, Stevie. And just for the record, in case you go off and get yourself killed again, I love you."

"I love you too, brother."

☽

I sleep so well in the aftermath of that tenderness. It stays with me in the emptiness and fullness of dreams and everything is soft and gentle and, for the first time in a very long time, very sweet. And so it's no surprise when I wake up this morning to the soft stroking of a hand on my cheek. No surprise because anything makes sense when crossing back to consciousness.

My eyes are still closed, savoring the sensation for just a moment longer.

The touch is as light as a feather.

It can't be Stevie. We are intimate but have never displayed affection like this.

It is not Mrs. Goldman. It is a younger hand.

I open my eyes and the woman staring back at me stirs up both a wave of confusion and a sudden gust of excitement.

"Skye," I say, calling to her through this window of disorientation. "What are you doing here?"

Twenty

Stevie appears in the doorway. He hovers. His eyes are narrow. There is worry on his face.

"Who died?" I ask.

Stevie shakes his head. "Nobody," he says, his voice trailing off as if it has somewhere else to go.

My sister looks on the verge of tears or laughter; her mouth scrunches up, her cheeks are red, her eyes scream through the silence. She could either be: a) witnessing a murder; or (b) enjoying an orgasm. But she's definitely containing something. I sit up. "What's wrong, Skye?"

"Nothing's wrong. Please get up. Get out of bed. I have something very important to tell you."

I eye Stevie. He looks away. I don't like this, and I make that very clear with an audible sigh as I swing my legs over the side of the bed and get up.

I follow Stevie to the kitchen, where Pensativa, the maid, is preparing a late breakfast for me. "*Gracias,*" I tell her. She smiles a bilingual smile and nods her head. Her skin is smooth and shiny.

I sit in front of my breakfast (huevos rancheros benedictos—don't ask—hash browns, mango juice, and hot tea) and my sister sits in front of me. Stevie is beside her.

"We have an announcement," she says. "We're in love."

My mouthful of mango juice, caught in an uncontrollable spasm of surprise, soars across the table and into her face. Stevie laughs. My sister does not as she wipes the pulp from her two-thousand-dollars-a-day cheekbones.

"In love?" I ask. "The two of you?"

"Yes," she replies.

"As in you're dating?"

"Seriously," she replies.

I turn to Stevie. My eyes say, *Oh, really?* but my lips say nothing. Stevie's face goes from red to pink to white. Sweat dampens his forehead.

This has to be a joke.

But I have the feeling it isn't.

Skye slides her hand across the table and grabs mine. "I just met the family last night, but we thought we'd wait until today to tell you."

I look away. I stare down at my plate. The huevos are running all over the ranchero and it looks like my breakfast is crying.

"You look upset," Skye says. "We thought you'd be thrilled."

"Did we?" I ask, fixing a man-to-man stare again at Stevie.

"I'm sorry," he finally says. "I'm really sorry I couldn't tell you before this."

"I'm really sorry I'm going to throw up all over the breakfast table," I tell him.

"Gray!" my sister cries.

I look at her and shake my head.

Do my eyes reveal the betrayal I feel? I wonder about that as I sit back and allow the estrangement to sink in. Me. And them. Them. Together. Without me. A new them. The old me. How the fuck did this happen?

Pensativa and her smile reenter the kitchen, and she moves her rounded figure to the table, where she drops me a puzzled if not offended look. "You no like?"

"Me gusta mucho. Pero no puedo comer mi desayuno."

"No tienes hambre."

"Ahora, no. Gracias."

She goes away.

"I'm sorry if we hurt your feelings," Stevie offers. "We've only been dating a few months, and we wanted to tell you all along, but I know how stressed out you've been, you know, over finding the murderer."

"That was very considerate of you both," I snap.

"Don't be like that," Skye begs me.

"Eat shit, Skyenerexia."

"Please, Graydove, try to understand. I love your sister. But I never meant for us to fall in love."

"Then how did it happen?"

"I was trying to help you, Gray."

"Trying to help *me*? While you were helping yourself to my baby sister? She's at least ten years younger than you, you know." I'm now reminded of Stevie's obsession with vagina. I know, for instance, that he loves cunnilingus. Instantly, I study my sister's face. I look for the same cunnilingual smile Stevie has left on so many faces before her.

It is there.

"I'm in my New York office a lot, you know," Stevie says. "I rang up Skye one day last year when I was in the city. We met for coffee. I tried to convince her to come back to Boston. To help you in your search for the killer. I knew how badly you wanted your family to help. I thought I could make that happen."

"So," I say to my sister, wincing as I take in, once again, that tunnel-of-love utterly satisfied grin of hers, "not only did you refuse to come back to Boston and help me out, you helped yourself to my best friend."

"That's not exactly what happened," she says. "I was so confused about Father's murder, Gray. Overcome with grief, really."

"And the rest of us were at a fucking luau?"

She *tsks* with a snap of her tongue. "No, Gray, that's not

what I'm saying. I didn't think I could handle going back to Boston. Stevie said he understood. He really listened to me. He was such a great comfort."

I shake my head and rise from the table. "So, you've been dating all this time. And keeping it your own dirty little secret."

"I've been seeing Skye every time I'm in New York, if that's what you mean."

"I mean by keeping it in the closet you've both deceived me. Both of you have had to plan and plot ways to keep this thing behind my back. Nothing could be more disrespectful to a brother and a *friend*!"

"We never lied to you," Skye says.

"Lying or hiding the truth? I'm not sure I know the difference. I don't like surprises. Not surprises like this."

"Gray," Stevie begs, "you just need to give this a chance and get used to the idea. My parents are thrilled. They love her."

"That's right," Skye whispers, and I think about the silhouetted tableau I witnessed last night from the outdoor spa as I contemplated the camel and the sky. She was there. Meeting the parents. Being welcomed warmly, probably adored.

This is very real.

I shrug. Does it really matter?

Skye looks at me expectantly.

So does her boyfriend.

"No, I'm not going to give this *relationship*"—the word tastes utterly rancid to me—"my blessing, just like that," I say with a snap of my fingers that irritates even me. "You don't get everything you want, everything you ask for, and then just sit back like some diva on a divan waiting for the world to get down and lick your—"

"Careful, Gray," Stevie warns.

"Toes."

"I don't know how you can even suggest that," Skye argues.

"I can suggest it, princess, because it's true. Now, if you want my blessing, you are going to get off your self-centered, everything's-about-me, coddle-me, pacify-me, worship-me ass and come to Boston where you belong and see your mother and take some goddamn responsibility like an adult."

"And then I get your blessing?" she gushes.

"I'm going out for a drive," I say, disgusted.

"Take the Jeep," Stevie says.

I don't reply. Instead I turn from the joyous couple, their faces all flush with new love and lusty satisfaction, and head back to my bedroom. I'm pursued down the hallway. I don't acknowledge the pursuer.

I enter the room and begin to change my clothes.

Stevie's voice is not far behind. "Hey, listen to me, Graydove," he says with collegiate freshness and eagerness. It's the same voice, the very exact voice I remember from all those years ago when we first encountered each other in the dorm laundry room. "Good to meet you," he said, the same sparkle in his handsome voice. "I'm Steven Goldman. Everyone calls me Stevie." The memory clutches my heart like a fist and shakes my insides with sadness and joy. When I turn, finally, to face my best friend in the doorway, tears are rolling down my face.

"Gray," he says, "you haven't lost your best friend. Chances are this will bring us closer."

I move quickly. Lace my shoes. Slap my baseball cap on my headful of morning hair and slide past Stevie Goldman.

I have to get out of here.

Twenty-One

I grab a map of Arizona and flee. Skye rushes to the door behind me. "Gray," she cries.

I ignore her, start the Jeep, and am gone.

I head east. I pass briefly through Scottsdale, and then I'm in the desert. The terrain changes dramatically and often. I'm surrounded by boulders now; I don't know how they stay like that, seemingly balanced atop one another, certain to tumble into traffic, but they don't. I think of other sacred places where Indian gods designed the landscapes, places like Machu Picchu where the spirits still whisper in the wind and control the order of things, and I realize that this landscape too—these unlikely stacks of boulders—is actually a very deliberate design. I imagine the gods coming out at night, re-arranging the boulders in ways so subtle as to change the picture without ever changing the impression. Perhaps that's how they entertain themselves. Whimsy.

The boulders disappear, and the land rolls, now flattened, and the cacti, all but the insistent prickly pear, disappear. Again the topography changes. Huge, sky-pounding, heart-pounding mountains hover around me. The road climbs, and twists, and turns.

I enter a town called Payson. A small town in higher terrain. Looks like New Hampshire or southern Vermont, abundant in pine and oak and fallen leaves. There is a distinct chill in the air. I'm surprised that the climate is so different here, only a couple of hours outside of Phoenix.

I see lots of signs for trail heads, but I'm reticent to forsake the Jeep for a solitary and perhaps dangerous hike. But the decision appears not to be mine. I am compelled—or, it seems, the Jeep is compelled—to turn off onto a dirt road, following signs for Fossil Creek.

The road ends. The trail begins. The trail descends into a canyon. I look across the wide, gaping hole at the high rim on the other side. Its colors change as it rises into the sky...stripes of green, stripes of slate, stripes of red. I walk downward. The bottom must be miles away. But I can't stop. The trail is clayish, lined with an unlikely pairing of prickly pear and pine. At times it is rocky and steep, precarious and unnerving. Every so often it flattens and gives me pause to consider the possibilities that space like this provides. Perhaps no one ever stood in this very spot before to contemplate the same thoughts as I. Surely no one ever stood here and worried about a best friend named Stevie and a sister named Skye and a dead father and a jailed mother and a boyfriend who wants to become a girlfriend.

I hear a gentle noise in the canyon below. It's either a brisk wind stirring through the trees or the rush of a mountain spring. I can't tell; this is, I suppose, nature being synonymous with itself. I continue my trek downward, taking my worries with me.

The openness of this place leaves me similarly vulnerable. A whoosh of possibilities swoops down on my neurotic head. I've gone over this a gazillion times. Backwards, forwards, in alphabetical order, in Spanish, French, and Motu (which I learned during a parking meter deal in Papua New Guinea), over coffee, between meals, during sex. And still again, I must review. Here, in the most compelling of silences, my uncooperative head is drilling—no, jackhammering—itself up my ass.

Father, oh, Father, who killed you?

I pause once more, thinking maybe I've missed a crack somewhere or overlooked a key discrepancy.

It's the same list as always: no suspects among the business associates, colleagues, partners, administrators. No love triangle. No adulterous secrets. No man wanting to get Father out of the way to get to Mother and her money. No blackmailers. No drug dealers. No political racketeering. No tennis racketeering either (this is only relevant because Father owned a small interest in a company that supplied the dyes for neon-colored tennis balls).

I'm down at the very bottom of the canyon, and at the end of my list. This has been fruitless. My only lead now is Bobby Bose. And I have serious and ugly doubts about that. I look up at the great sky. I'm dwarfed by the huge rim around me and the umbrella of flawless cerulean blue. I stretch out my arms to embrace this gift of God, and I feel my Indian ancestry joining my hands and giving me lift and promise. I'm tingling all over, and I can hear their voices now, the natives who found magic in these canyons and saw in the eyes of their gods that this is where they were supposed to be. It is what it is. You are what you are. Father always said those words to me. Prefaced by nothing else, predicated by nothing more. And this, finally, is where I understand the depth and possibility of what he meant.

Father, I miss you.

Is that enough, or must I find your killer?

A light wind rustles around me. It's an autumn wind, not unlike the crisp touch of November in New England. But the sun, streaming in abstract slants through a forest of branches, hits my face, and it is Arizona warm. I follow a stream as it grows mightier and frothier, and I watch as it dumps into a pool so clear I can see straight down into the stony bottom.

I want to be naked in the clarity of this water, so I strip down and jump in, and the chill tickles my armpits and my navel and my anus all at once. I shiver, but then I swim about, and the water rocks me gently until I'm warm.

Dried off, I pull my clothes back on and begin what turns

out to be an arduous climb out of the canyon. It's steep at first, and I lose my breath. I worry for a moment about passing out all alone here in the desperate isolation of this empty place. But then I remember the faith I have in the spirits around me and I trudge onward. At one point—I'm not sure which point—the trek becomes effortless. My legs, my heart, my lungs have adjusted to the exertion, and I'm moving freely, as if the rocks below my feet are springs vaulting me upward.

I'm driving back at the peak and fall of sunset. The mountains are brilliant in the orange dust of dusk. At times it seems these mountains glow, not from the coronation of a sinking sun, but from inside themselves. The pinks and the golds and the oranges and the yellows seem to come from a fire inside, a heartbeat that tells you these beasts are alive long after dark.

Suddenly I laugh. The tall saguaro cacti line the road back, hundreds, thousands of them, standing now in silhouette against the dimming sky. Most have one stalk thrust straight up high, with shorter stalks growing out at either side. It occurs to me that this scenery looks like a desertful of cacti giving me the finger all the way home.

☽

Pensativa is in the kitchen, her busy hands mixing like a blender over the final preparations for dinner. The family is already seated. They are taken by surprise by my entrance; I'm greeted by cautious smiles. Their collective sigh of relief steams up the glassware.

"Hi" slips through my lips. I don't say much else. I know this confuses them; they don't know whether to feel forgiven or to make more excuses for their behavior.

Pensativa arrives with beautiful salads. I see her pride in the way she swoops into the room, the way the tray fills her arms, the way she confidently puts a bowl down in front of each of us. She is a performance artist of sorts; food is her medium.

There is much chewing.

There is sipping of wine.

Forks *ping* as knives divide and conquer.

There is some conversation. And I am like the kid in gym trying to avoid the ball.

After dinner we drift into Mr. Goldman's study, a room of many levels, befitting an architect, with drawing boards and perfect halos of light, work stations for different projects, wood, enamel, glass block, charcoal-gray fixtures.

We gather around an easel shrouded in cloth. Mr. Goldman swipes the cloth away, revealing his latest aviation expression:

PLEASE DO NOT SPEAK TO SURROUNDING
PASSENGERS UNLESS SPOKEN TO FIRST

No one says a word. We continue to stare. Mr. Goldman smiles, anticipating a response. Finally, he urges us. "What do you think?" he asks.

"It's wonderful, Dad," Stevie says. "Really, it is."

Mrs. Goldman folds her arms across her chest and gives her husband a proud, approving look. "Well, it's about time someone put it in writing."

Skye looks at me nervously. I look away.

"What about you, Gray? What do you think?" Mr. Goldman asks.

Oh, shit. "With all due respect, I think it sounds a bit severe."

"Really?"

"Well, I think we should encourage human contact, not find ways to avoid it."

Mr. Goldman tilts his head, as if considering the notion,

but then dismisses it just as quickly. "Oh, but Gray, perhaps the sign itself will serve as a conversation piece. People will read it, laugh about it, and it will break the ice for true, friendly dialogue between passengers."

He delivers this last idea like a conductor with a baton. His arms are a-swing with the beat, the energy, the genesis of something new, vibrant, and, God almighty, profitable.

"Boeing has already ordered four hundred thousand," his voice crescendos.

"Oh, darling, I'm so proud!" Mrs. Goldman cries.

"Me too, Dad. Me too," Stevie adds.

I see how the game is played here with the family Goldman. I see how it is played and I see how it works, and, as I've always suspected, it is much different than the family Hoffenstein.

"How soon will we be seeing your new signs on board, Dad?"

"Real soon, Stevie. They'll be right above the folding tray tables. To the left of TRAY TABLE MUST BE STOWED FOR TAKE-OFF AND LANDING. To the right of YOUR SEAT CUSHION MAY BE USED AS A FLOTATION DEVICE."

"Imagine that," I say. "There's a business for everything."

"Congratulations," Skye offers.

"With any luck, the foreign rights will sell immediately."

And we all start to laugh. Within one microsecond of one another we all burst into laughter because we all know the story of the translation mishap some years ago when Mr. Goldman sold the rights to his PLEASE WIPE THE WASH BASIN AS A COURTESY TO THE NEXT PASSENGER sign to a Japanese airline. Seems that the translator got confused and an entire fleet of Japanese jets carried lavatory signs asking travelers to PLEASE WIPE THE NEXT PASSENGER AS A COURTESY.

Oh, how we laugh. And oh, how tired I am after my arduous hike into a strange and spiritual canyon. I politely withdraw from the room, wishing everyone a pleasant evening and a good night's sleep.

Stevie winces at my formality.

Skye follows me to my room.

"Gray..."

"Not now, Skye, I'm exhausted."

"Where were you all day? We were worried."

"I was fine. Found a wonderful place to be alone."

"I want to tell you something."

"Can't it wait until morning? Or next week? Or maybe Pesach?"

"No, it can't. I want you to know that I'm coming home with you."

Sitting at the side of the bed, I untie my shoes and let them drop to the floor. "Oh?"

"Yes. I'll stay around as long as you'd like me to. I'll visit Mother. I'll visit her as often as she can stand me."

I look up and see her eyes are filling. She is genuine. I just know. Maybe Stevie has gotten to her. If no one else can, he can. Maybe I should be thankful that she found him, that she will have his influence. "Mother can stand you," I tell my baby sister. "Often."

Twenty-Two

I ask Stevie and Skye to stay with me in the penthouse. I think this is a very grand gesture toward acceptance, but I do not articulate this. Unfortunately, the grandest gestures must be left unspoken or they become scorecards.

They accept.

(I score.)

Skye immediately eyes the hallway toward the master bedroom suite.

I shake my head no. She places her hands on her hips.

"There are plenty of other bedrooms in this place, Skye."

"Not with a spa."

"You're more than welcome to use my spa, as long as Pedro and I aren't in there."

"Where's the boyfriend?" she asks.

"Must be at rehearsal," I reply.

The phone rings.

"Maybe it's him," she says.

It isn't. It's my boss.

"Ben. How are you?"

"Fine," he says curtly. "You're planning on coming back to work sometime?"

I shake my head and release some pressure from my chest and shoulders in the form of a deep exhale. "Of course. I'm about to leave for the office now."

"I thought you'd be here when I got back from the business trip."

"I told you I'd be in Phoenix."

"You might have. But my mind has been on one thing only, Gray."

"Work?"

"No."

"Your marriage?"

"No."

"The Celtics?"

"Uh-uh."

"Oh."

"You, Gray, you. I must see you. We must finish where we left off."

"Left off?"

I know the answer.

"The airport. The...kiss," he says.

It's the answer I expected. I clear my throat. "We need to talk. And this isn't the time. I'll be in soon."

I'm off the phone. I turn around and Stevie and Skye are gone. Off to find a suitable bedroom, I'm sure. I pull some linens and towels from the closet in the hallway. I listen for their voices and carry the bundle toward the room they've chosen. I open the door, and they are oblivious to my entrance. Perhaps it's because Stevie's back is to me, his naked ass pumping madly into the crevice created by my sister's parted legs.

My sister doesn't look up. Her head is buried in his neck. She's chomping on his shoulder.

Apparently the sex they were denied during a five-hour flight could not wait a second longer. They make porno-movie groans; my sister's voice actually changes during sex. It raises an octave or two and sounds almost birdlike. What a range! Stevie's ass looks as in-shape as ever. Round, symmetrical bubble cheeks, just a shade lighter than his torso and legs. He is plowing into my sister, raiding her garden like a pirate on an island of treasure.

Ahh.
Ohh.
Oooh.
Aaaah.
Eee.
Eee.
Now.
Now?
Yeah, now!
Wait.
I can't.
Oh, God, please wait.
Ah-huh.
Yeah.
Oh, baby.
That's better.
Ergggggghhhhhiiiiiii.
Ayeyiyiyiyi.
Ooh. OOh. OOH.
Uh. UH. UHH.
Fiuskjepcnoaliwnnssj!
BBBDEDJKOOJDJDHKALKY!
CBBBSOOOOHHHHKSKKMMALIOQL!

I leave the room completely unnoticed—and not the least bit aroused—though somewhat curious as to my own carnal language.

I drive to work. I picture mad, relentless, acrobatic sex with Ben. I am in deep trouble:

a) I'm in a committed relationship (albeit with a man on the verge of becoming a woman).

b) Ben is my boss.

c) Ben is my boss.

d) Ben is still married.

e) Ben might fire me if I do or if I don't.

f) Am I being sexually harassed?

g) And if I am, why do I see Ben burying the smooth shaft of his hard dick deep inside my anal pore?

I park my car in the company garage, those mixed feelings bubbling in my head, that carnal image stirring me in my loins, the keys shaking in my hand.

The elevator (again, I am thinking *shaft*) lifts me to the seventeenth floor. I enter the office and nod politely, smile, say a few hellos to the secretarial pool. They are, well, *secretarial* again. The boss is back. Their sparkle is gone. They wear polyester again. They do not smile. They wear careless makeup that is all but soaked up by the fluorescence of the yellow room.

Poor them.

"Gray, I need to see you."

It's Ben.

Poor me.

He shuts the door behind me.

He stand there and smiles.

We are three feet away from each other; no one's circle is invaded. Yet.

"I've thought of you the entire time," he tells me. "And nothing else."

"How were the meetings, Ben? Anything new to report?"

"Nothing compared to you."

"Ben..."

"I'm serious, Gray."

"So am I. You went off for the most important meetings of the year and all you thought of was me?"

"Is there anything else?"

"Your wife?"

"Divorce."

"Who wants it?"

"Both of us."

"It will be very public, especially if anyone finds out about the gay thing."

"What gay thing?"

"That you're divorcing because you're gay."

He steps closer, reaches his hand out. "Let me explain something, Gray. I'm divorcing Marla because she's a cheating, scheming prima donna. She counts the seconds her face is on the air, and if her coanchor gets to read more lines or has one more second on the goddamned screen than she, she goes into a spectacular rage and is dangerous to be around. She says she doesn't get enough *face time*! Can you believe it? She was never in it for the news, you know, the *journalism* of it all."

"Face time?"

"Yeah, face time! These anchorpeople actually worry about whose face gets more time on the air."

"You're kidding."

"No, it's an ego thing."

"You really hate her."

"No, I really don't."

"Sure sounds like you do."

He turns to the window and the view outside. It's pretty for a late-fall day, even though the first eternally gray skies hover over Boston. The foliage is gone, having peaked tremendously for a week or two and then faded into the history of seasons like the way leaves find themselves pressed into the wax pages of children's scrapbooks.

"I hate myself more than I hate Marla," he says, studying the memory of color. I can see his reflection in the glass in front of him. It's thoughtful and serious, and I do believe his bottom lip quivers a bit. "I was a practicing homosexual before I met her."

I'm somewhat shocked. "You were practicing to be a homosexual?" I ask, trying to get him to abandon the view and face me. It works.

"No, Gray. I was actually gay. But then I met her and fell in love with her stardom."

"Stardom, shmardom, Ben. She's a *local anchorwoman.* Big fucking deal. She's not Barbara Walters, for chrissake. She's not even Connie What-the-Hell-Happened-to-Me Chung."

"But what gay man doesn't worship a diva? Even a *local* diva..."

I contemplate this and then say, "Yes, I suppose I'll allow you that."

"I love you, Gray."

I sit. I'm swallowing his words and they are clogging my throat and blocking words of my own from coming out. What if I just sit here and gag? I wonder. Do I change the subject? Do I pretend not to hear and say, "Excuse me"? Do I say, "Excuse me, I'm passing a kidney stone"?

"Gray..."

"Ben..."

"Gray?"

"Ben?"

"Say something," he begs.

"I think you must be mistaken."

"Mistaken?"

"Yes, Ben, mistaken. You think I'm the answer for you. You're hurting for the betrayal you feel and all those years you lost living a life you weren't meant to live, and here I am, a gay man you feel comfortable with, and well, it's only natural that you mistake this comfort and longing for love."

"Shut up, Gray. I'm in love with you."

I shake my head. Vigorously. This makes me incredibly dizzy, so I grip the chair handles. "No, you're not. Don't do this to yourself. You are not in love with me."

"I'm so attracted to you," he says, putting his head in his hands.

"But you're not in love with me. Wanting to fuck me is not the same thing as being in love."

"I'm attracted to who you are, Gray. Don't you see that? I've wanted to fuck you from the moment I hired you, but now I know I've fallen in love."

Jesus Christ.

Holy Moses.

Dear Fucking Abby.

"I'm in a relationship, Ben. You know that."

He's silent. The truth is quelling. I think.

A phone buzzes. He presses a button and asks his secretary to take messages. Over the speaker phone, she assures him in a wet lipstick voice that she will.

"Pedro?" he asks.

"Yes."

"Do you love him?"

"Ben, I'm not having this discussion with you."

"You don't, do you?"

"Of course I love Pedro." And at this moment I sense very deeply that I do.

"But you're having problems...right?"

"That's none of your business."

"I can tell by your disposition lately. Things are not so cozy in the penthouse."

"Ben, please, stop. I think I should probably resign if this is going to cause such a problem."

His eyes almost slay me. "No! You can't do that! You're my best accountant. I need to have you around."

"So you can sit in here and fantasize about something that's not going to happen?"

"You're cruel," he tells me.

"I'm sorry. I'm honest. That's all."

He is so damn good-looking. I remember now the flavor of his skin against mine during that ferocious and fleeting airport kiss He smelled musky and masculine, and I swear I could taste the sweat of his thighs in that one brief inhalation of him. This is way too much. I rise quickly and make for the door.

"Gray?"

"Gotta run," I say. "Been away too long, lots to catch up on."

"We'll finish this later," he calls to me.

"It's finished, Ben," I muster. "It's finished."

I swing the door open and nearly collide with Wet Lipstick Voice, who is standing on the other side. Has she been listening? Has she been gathering gossip? Does she think we fucked? Instinctively I check my fly, and she notices this, which makes matters worse.

"I'm sorry," she says. "I was just on my way in. You've got a call, Gray. It sounds urgent."

I take the call at my desk.

It's Chaka. She's sobbing heavily. She tells me something and I go numb. The blood just flushes right out of my head. Time and space, mind and body are paralyzed.

The news is bad.

Brenda Cloudholder is dead.

Twenty-Three

"Dead?"

"Dead."

"Just like that?"

"Just like what...?"

"Form of speech, Chaka."

"Yes, of course. I don't have many details. I just got a frantic call from Derderva. The poor man is absolutely devastated."

"And that cat...she must be lost without Brenda."

"The other way around, Gray. The other way around. As it happens, it's a blessing Brenda went first. Had Lourdes up and died, Brenda would have no one to steer her through life."

"I suppose you're right," I concede. "Was it a heart attack? A stroke?"

"I don't know. Derderva's so shaken up he couldn't say much. I told him we'd fly in tonight."

"Oh?"

"We will. Won't we?"

"I...guess."

"Gray? Is this a problem? After all Brenda has done for us?"

"No," I assure my sister. "It's just that I really shouldn't be taking any more time off from work. I just got back from Phoenix last night. I haven't even read the morning paper."

"You haven't?" she asks, sounding jolted.

"Nope."

"Oh..."

"Why? What is it?"

"Oh, nothing," she lies. I can tell.

"C'mon, I'm sure there's a paper lying around the office here somewhere. If you don't tell me, I'll just go read it for myself."

"Oh, it's probably nothing, but they think Stevie's plane was sabotaged."

I'm stunned, but having been stunned by Brenda's death, I'm already too numb to completely feel this latest surprise. Instead I feel a moderate sense of wow. "Who's *they*?" I ask my sister.

"They. I dunno. The FAA. The NTSB. Whoever. Hasn't Stevie read the paper?"

"No," I snicker. "He's too busy fucking—never mind."

"Well, they're going to want to talk to him, I'm sure."

"Whoever *they* are."

"Oh, Gray, stop being so goddamn difficult."

"I'm sorry. It's been a very eventful morning so far. Book us a flight on PBA. We can fly over this afternoon. Ben will just have to understand."

"I hope he doesn't fire you."

"I don't think there's any chance of that," I tell her. "Look, I'll run home and pack a bag. We'll stay on the island tonight. But let's make it an early flight back in the morning."

"Don't you think you'd better get in touch with Stevie before we leave?" she asks.

"Don't worry. I'll see him at the penthouse. He's staying there."

"At the penthouse? Why?"

"Long story."

"Are you...and he...you know?"

"Shut up, Chaka. Call me when you get us a flight."

She hangs up. I hang up. I offer a brief, detached explanation to Ben and I am gone.

❩

The penthouse is quiet, save for human sounds coming from the master bedroom suite. *My* master bedroom suite. They wasted no time. They're fucking in the spa. I just know it. I follow the sounds of laughter and grunts and the sweaty smell of lovers at play; it's been sex all day, I'm sure.

My spa is so steamed up I can barely see their naked forms, but I do make out the mountain of foam heaving from the hot tub and am both confused and concerned.

"I don't think you're supposed to make a bubble bath in a hot tub," I call to them.

Suddenly the sounds of sex cease and I am standing there, the steam clearing, surrounded by fuck bubbles.

"Gray?"

"No, the French lieutenant's woman. Of course it's me."

"Sorry," Stevie says.

"Sorry," Skye squeaks.

I tell them they'll have all night to foam-fuck as I must make a dash for the Vineyard. I share the sad news of Brenda's death, and at first Stevie insists he must join me. After all, he argues, he's been as much a part of these encounters with Brenda as anybody else. But then I tell him about the report in the morning paper, and suddenly he leaps from the hot tub, dripping in foam, his semihard penis purple and raw. There's no way that can feel good, I assure myself, warding off the claws of jealousy reaching for the back of my neck.

"Sabotage!"

"I brought the paper home from work. It's in the foyer."

He dashes from the spa.

"Please don't track foam through the penthouse," I call to him.

Skye is toweling herself off, looking mighty proud and somewhat embarrassed at the same time. She is a beautiful girl, my sister. I can see why Stevie fell for her and why she sometimes actually does get paid to have her picture taken.

"Oh, my God!" It's Stevie. He has returned, completely flaccid, to the spa.

"What?" I beg.

"You're right. They think it was sabotage!" he cries. "Who would want to kill me? Who would want to destroy my plane?"

"What about your Jesse Helms theory?"

"Shush, Gray. I'm serious."

"So am I."

"My theory was wrong. If someone is going to go to all the trouble to sabotage a plane, if someone is going to take that much of a risk, they're not going to mix up whose plane is whose."

"I think you'd better talk to the investigators."

"The FAA?"

"Yes, Stevie," I reply.

"Shit! Maybe that's why my office has been paging me all day."

My sister pouts. The pout is guilt-ridden but obligatory. Apparently she and her vagina are why Stevie has ignored the pages.

Naked, Stevie calls his office and finds that the FAA and the NTSB have indeed been looking for him since yesterday afternoon, before the story got leaked to the media.

"They want to question me," he tells us.

"Of course they do," I say.

"They may want to question you too, Gray."

"Me? Why?"

"Because you were on board when things started going wrong."

"So?"

"They'll want to know that I didn't sabotage the plane, myself. You know, to collect the insurance..."

"Right, of course," I assure him. "Why would you sabotage your own plane if you knew we would be flying it...?"
"Exactly, Gray. All this detective work is really paying off for you."
No, it isn't.
He laughs.
I don't.
He gets dressed. The entire penthouse smells like honeysuckle foam bath and orgasm.
I *am* jealous.
"I've got to get to the airport," Stevie says.
"I'm meeting Chaka at Logan," I tell him. "You can go with me."
He agrees.
Skye throws herself on the tempting red satin claw-foot couch and whimpers. "What about me?"
"What about you?" I ask.
"What will I do? Where do I fit in to all this excitement?"
Stevie ignores her, and I am proud of him.
"You don't fit in," I tell my sister. "We love you, but you don't fit in right now."
"Then what do you expect me to do with myself?"
"I would suggest something fairly obvious, but I'm certain you're rather sore down there."
"Gray..." Stevie warns.
"I'm serious!" my sister cries. "You can't just leave me here."
I'm tossing clothes into a duffel bag. "Of course we can."
She groans.
"I have one suggestion," I tell her. "You can go to the prison and visit Mother."
"Mother?"
"Yes, you know. Our mother, the inmate?"
She looks at me nervously and shakes her head slowly. "Oh...I don't know, Gray."
"You made me a promise."

"Promise?"

"That you'd go see Mother as often as possible."

"Yes, I did. But aren't you going to give me a few days to assimilate back into Boston?"

I laugh and wince. "It's not like you came here from the Ukraine."

"But you didn't tell me I'd have to go out and visit Mother alone."

"No, I didn't. But you do. I'll leave you money for a cab."

I zip up my duffel. Stevie finishes dressing. I call Chaka and tell her I am tired of waiting, that we need to get on the next flight and get this done with.

"No problem, brother," she tells me. "I'm leaving for the airport now. Everything was booked, so I chartered us a plane."

"You what?"

"Chartered a plane. Mother and Father used to do it all the time."

"Oh, God. How much did this cost?"

"I don't know, a few thousand dollars."

"Fuck. This Brenda lady is really costing us a lot of money. Even in death."

"This is no time to argue, Gray. We have a dear friend who's gone and died on us. And a medium, no less. Who do you think will work with us now? Another medium? Huh? Did you ever think of that?"

"No, Chaka. I never thought of that."

"Meet me at Standard Aviation."

"I'm leaving now."

Twenty-Four

I can't see water.

I can't see land.

I can't see how this pilot is going to land this plane.

A long, silky robe of fog hangs over the Vineyard. My first inquiry ("Are you sure it's safe to descend?") to our pilot, a Norwegian-looking man named Spinkus, is ignored. He has a strong jawline and fearless eyes. I do not. I'm scared for my life, and Chaka is dry-heaving in the seat behind me. Spinkus (first or last name, I do not know, and to ask right now might force him to take his eyes of the valley of soup in front of us that he can't see through anyway) is a former military man, I guess, the kind of pilot who won't let zero visibility get in the way of a good landing. He's wearing a light, springy cologne with a trace of fresh pine. Very inappropriate for these grave circumstances, if I do say so myself.

I imagine the ghost of Brenda Cloudholder (perhaps she'd prefer *spirit* to *ghost*) is somewhere in the fog in front of us. Perhaps Brenda is actually guiding us in safely by a leash. No, she's blind. That won't work.

I wonder if she regained her eyesight on the other side.

I wonder much in this quiet and calm interlude between life and almost certain death.

"You can't see, Sphincter, can you?" Chaka asks.

"Spinkus!" he corrects her. "And, as a matter of fact, I can see. Not with the naked eye, of course. But all these fancy instruments are like a second pair of eyes."

I don't believe him. I know enough about aviation to know we should be diverting to Hyannis.

He reads my mind. "I would turn back for Hyannis," he says. "But I don't have enough fuel."

That soothes my mind. Not.

We continue to descend, and I expect that we will either: a) glide into a fixed object somewhere (a lighthouse, cliff, a passenger ferry); or b) hit the ground, splat, like a bug on a windshield.

This is not a multiple-choice proposition, but Spinkus picks option "b" and, splat, we hit something (the runway?), surge forward, squeal, squeak, and all but give the ground an episiotomy to come to a stop.

It's so foggy I can't even see the shack they call a terminal. It's so foggy the ground crew says "Congratulations" to our smiling pilot, which is a source of some discomfort to me.

The Yugo is waiting.

Derderva shakes my hand, hugs my sister. His skin is pasty. Dark circles surround his eyes. The car has a very good stereo, it seems—for a Yugo. We are listening to opera at high volume. *La Traviata,* I think. I don't speak Italian, so I'm not sure. Chaka rolls down her backseat window and throws up.

Derderva lowers the stereo and turns to her. "Are you okay, Ms. Hoffenstein?"

She nods her head as she wipes her chin.

"You don't have to be so formal with us," I tell him.

He offers a thin smile.

"We've come to help you with the arrangements, you know."

He won't look at me, but he nods and whispers, "Thank you, I thought so."

"Anything you need, Derderva, you let us know. And if you'd rather stay with us at Sea Valley, you're more than welcome," Chaka says.

I wince an invisible wince but figure, okay, what the hell, the guy's in pain. "Sure," I add unconvincingly.

"No, no. I'll stay at Brenda's. Things need to be done."

"As you wish," Chaka tells him. "Did she die in her sleep?"

"She did," he replies.

"Was it a heart attack?" my sister inquires.

The man's eyes are moist with tears now. "That's what the doctors think. That's what they assume."

"Are they doing an—"

"Chaka, really, this isn't the time for a lot of questions," I say.

"That's okay," Derderva tells us. "They're not doing any kind of tests on her, if that's what you mean. She's a person who would like her spirit to leave in peace."

"Her weight probably didn't help much," my sister persists. "She was a heavy woman."

I turn to Chaka and force a glare that, in some countries without parking meters, would be considered a lethal weapon. She shrugs and lips "Fuck you" to me.

"Yes, she was heavy," Derderva concedes. "And she never did much to restrict her diet." His tone has changed as he waxes, it seems, nostalgic. "I mean, the woman could down a gallon of Ben and Jerry's in one sitting..."

"Couldn't we all?" I suggest.

"Not me," Derderva says. "I'm lactose intolerant."

Suddenly, this odd man who I have always known as so aloof, so ambiguously detached, seems very human. He looks no different, just somewhat humbled, perhaps less Lurch-like than before. Admitting you get diarrhea from ice cream can do this to a man, I guess.

At last, *Entre Tetas*. Once a servant, always a servant, Derderva carries our bags inside (this, despite our, well, *my* protest). Chaka collapses in the family room; we seem to be purposefully avoiding the formal parlor, where all the séances have been held, either out of collective and unspoken respect for Brenda Cloudholder or out of fear. Real summer-camp-ghost-story, haunted-house kind of fear. I wonder, though, if the parlor is not on some kind of autopilot, ready to séance as soon as a mortal enters the room.

I ask Derderva if I can borrow the Yugo to get some groceries. He tells me not to bother. He has stocked the kitchen. I am surprised; I ask him how he got into the house without a key. He leaves the room without answering, returning moments later with a pitcher of lemonade.

"No, thank you," I tell him.

My sister holds her pregnant and nauseated stomach and shakes her head, no, emphatically.

"I have more proof Bobby Bose killed your father," he says dryly.

The announcement forces my sister from the sofa to her feet. She gasps. "What!"

I'm calmer. "Derderva? Are you serious? Please..."

He nods and sits in a high wingback chair in front of the window. The light behind him, however feeble, darkens his face and makes reading his eyes, his expression, almost fruitless. "I wanted to wait until I got you here to Sea Valley before I told you."

My sister retreats to the sofa and sits. "And, so?"

"I finally found what I was looking for," the bereaved servant continues. "The airlines weren't so willing to hand over old manifests, you know. But I know everybody at that airport. *Everybody.* I went through every single flight, every single day for two weeks before and two weeks after Mr. Hoffenstein's death. And now I know exactly which flights Bobby took in and out of here."

"It's circumstantial evidence," I say, "at best."

"You can convict on circumstantial evidence, Graydove," Derderva explains, "at least in Massachusetts."

"Well, with all due respect, I still don't see how this advances anything. You've told us before about tracking Bobby Bose to the Vineyard."

"Well, now we know he was here two days before your father's murder and left the day after his body was found. And we also know where he stayed."

"And?" Chaka begs.

"And I can place Bobby Bose at an Oak Bluffs guesthouse on those very same evenings," Derderva chants with the expertise of a detective.

"No!" Chaka cries.

"Yes."

"I don't know," I say. "Don't forget we have it on a higher authority that Bobby didn't do it."

"That's right! Grandmother Hoffenstein!" Chaka cries, pointing to the ceiling. She considers the air above her for a moment, swishes around a suspicious notion and then, soberly, says, "But maybe Grandmother is wrong."

Something falls in the kitchen.

A door slams.

My sister looks at me nervously. Her eyes dart from side to side. "Then again, maybe not," she says. "But could it be just a coincidence that Bobby was here when Father was murdered? Believe me, I'd love for it not to be true."

"I'm afraid it is," Derderva says calmly. "The owners of the Salt House Inn recognized him right away."

"Recognized him?" Chaka asks. "How?"

"I have photos."

"Photos?"

"Pictures, rather...hmm, how shall I say—pictorial?"

The color disappears from Chaka's face. "The *Playgirl* pictures?"

Derderva smiles meekly. "They were the only ones I could get my hands on."

I catch on. I'm so amused my cheeks hurt from bracing my entire face against an explosion of laughter that would surely result in a whack upside the head from my humiliated sister. "The El Camino pictures," I summarize.

"Exactly," Derderva says.

"Oh...my...God!" Chaka cries. "You showed every innkeeper on this island those pictures?"

"Just about," he replies. "He has a rather large penis."

"I know," Chaka says reflectively, then maddens. "How could you spread that awful magazine with all those awful pictures all over this island?"

"People have seen it, Chaka," I remind her. "This entire island sold out of it in two days. Remember?"

"I mean, that is one of the largest penises I've ever seen," Derderva tells us.

"I can assure you the innkeepers would have recognized him by his face ONLY," my sister insists.

"Surely," he concedes. "But boy, it's a big one."

"Enough," I suggest politely. "The question is what do we do now?"

Derderva leans forward. "Clearly, this Bobby Bose had the opportunity to kill Colin Hoffenstein. And from the sounds of it, he must have had a means and a motive. Ask any cop. That's all you need."

"I suppose we should share this news with Detective Plotzman," I think aloud.

"Maybe so," says Derderva with a quirky grin. "But the real question is why did this family keep Bobby Bose a secret all this time? Why didn't you go to the police about Bobby when your father was first killed? Everything I found out the police could have found out within days of the murder. Your poor mother might never have been arrested. I think Detective Plotzman will want an explanation."

It feels as though Derderva has assumed Brenda's surrogacy and become, well, parental toward us.

"We had no reason to," I tell him. "It never occurred to any of us to consider him a suspect."

"Oh, I thought about it," Chaka says with a warble in her voice. "But...but...I couldn't bring myself to believe it was possible. I couldn't accept even the passing thought that my marriage was responsible for Father's murder."

"And I was totally convinced, or rather, Kirkland had me totally convinced the murder had something to do with the family money," I explain. "And you have to understand, Derderva, it took nearly a year for the shock of this whole thing to wear off. We were numb. Just numb. And then the next thing you know, Mother's on trial."

"Well, I think the detective will understand all this," Derderva assures us.

Chaka is choking on tears.

She cries and cries. "Father would still be alive if I hadn't forced Bobby on the family. Mother wouldn't be in jail. What was I thinking? I'll never ever be able to live with myself."

"Please, Chaka," I beg, "don't do this to yourself. Remember, we don't have proof Bobby killed anybody. Just because he was here doesn't mean he murdered Father."

Chaka flees from the room.

Derderva rises from the chair. Only now do I realize how wiry and agile he is. There is a certain precision in his movement; he has the posture of a ballet dancer, the balance of a beam-walking gymnast. His age is a mystery. Perhaps he discovered moisturizers very early in life. I wonder. He moves to the front door in an elegant way. "She loved you both, you know."

I look at him, surprised.

"She did. She thought of you and Chaka as very special. She loved that you loved your father enough to go to all these efforts. She once told me that if she had had children she would have wanted them to be like you and Norma Lee."

I can do nothing but nod and shake the man's hand.

"Don't forget the lemonade," he tells me. "I made it fresh."

I attempt a smile, but the sorrow quivering at my lip is stronger than my will. I close the door and listen as the man's footsteps lead him to the waiting Yugo.

I am touched and moved to tears.

Twenty-Five

I must confess. I didn't sleep well last night (that merits a confession only in the sense that I normally boast about how life on the Vineyard lulls me to sleep—and that's about all I boast about, since *Entre Tetas* in all its grandeur speaks for itself); between my tears for Brenda and the disturbing sounds from downstairs, I tossed and turned and would not be pacified. Not by the usual rock-a-bye rhythm of the ocean, or the healing salt air, or the stillness of an off-season stars-to-ourselves night.

The noises persisted all evening. Not the kind of noises that make me clutch the covers right below my frightened eyelids as if the place were haunted. The place *is* haunted. I know this. I accept this.

It wasn't Father (he seems reticent to appear, and I'm beginning to wonder, in fact, if he's truly dead or whether he simply staged his murder and fled to a Native American, Jewish commune—a kibbutz with a casino—somewhere north of San Francisco), and it wasn't Grandmother (I know her moccasin-padded footsteps like I know the back of my hand and all the others I've held at these many séances). And I don't think it was Brenda Cloudholder, though I did begin to wonder about that possibility, given the sounds of so many things being knocked over—things falling from the kitchen counters, it seemed, and from bookshelves in the library too. It would make sense, would it not, that a woman who lived blind and died blind would move about blind in the afterlife, bumping into everything even in the friendliest of hauntings.

But why the lemons?

I am confused by the lemons.

After wrestling with the "should I, could I, may I, can I go back to sleep" psychodrama, I finally decided to unscramble myself from the bed covers, pull on last night's socks, sweatpants, and a robe, and head for the kitchen, perhaps make coffee, see if the smell of it rouses Chaka from bed like it does for all those Folgers families on television.

I push the kitchen door open only to find, much to my surprise, a floor covered with lemons, not unlike a ball-strewn tennis court in the wake of furious and foul volleys. I am careful and confused. Careful to watch my step lest I catch a heel on one of the yellow fruits and go flying across the industrial-size kitchen, landing, with my luck, headfirst into one of the steel freezer doors. At first I'm confused by the mere presence of lemons in the kitchen. (Why are they here? Who brought them? Are they in season?) Then I remember the lemonade. Yes, the lemonade. Derderva was kind enough to leave us a pitcherful in the drawing room to refresh us upon our arrival, and neither Chaka nor I bothered to have even a sip. I enter the drawing room, find the pitcher, and return to the kitchen, where I pour the now-stale lemonade into the sink. As I do this, the lemons on the floor begin to shimmy like the breasts of Vegas showgirls. I look again and the fruit is shaking about, as if a fault line has shifted beneath *Entre Tetas,* making one *teta* go this way, one *teta* go the other way.

I leave the kitchen.

For Chaka, the best part of waking up will not be Folgers in her cup. Instead I pull at the blankets bunched up around her feet.

"What?" she groans.

"Get up."

"Why?"

"You have to see something."

"Can you bring it here?"

"Not possible."

She gets up.

I show her the lemons.

She gasps, holding her hands to her mouth, like a teeth-chattering little girl on a frigid winter day.

"It's weird," I say.

"No shit."

I tell her about the noises I heard all night.

"Didn't hear a thing," she says. "Black people sleep heavier."

"You're not black, and they do not."

"Well, I didn't hear anything. I sleep heavier than you."

"Do you think we can have a séance without Brenda?"

"We might have to."

The phone rings.

"I'll get it in the drawing room," I say.

Chaka follows.

It's Pedro.

"Just wanted to make sure you're coming back for my show," he says.

I hesitate, searching for the language of diplomacy. "Surely, Pedro, you understand that with Brenda's death, well, there are things that need to be done."

"Things?"

"There's a private service tomorrow. We'll need to stay."

"But the show's not till the day after tomorrow. You can still make it back."

"Yes, I suppose we can."

"Stevie and Skye will be there. They told me they will be. You know they're here at the penthouse."

"Yes. Forgot to let you know. Sorry."

"Don't be, *precioso*. They're letting me rehearse for them."

"We'll be back for your show," I tell him.

"Promise?"

"Promise."

Chaka and I return to the kitchen to bag the lemons and store them in a food chest, only to find that the fruit is now all lined up and arranged to form the letter *J*.

"J?" Chaka asks.

"J," I repeat.

"Someone is playing a nasty joke on us," she says.

"I don't know. A joke has a punch line. This doesn't. This seems more like a trick."

"Or a message..." she says with spooky eyes.

"A message? Like what? 'When life gives you lemons, make lemonade'?"

Chaka smiles, gladly chewing on the possibility. "Sure," she says. "I've got it."

"I don't. No ghost we know would send us a sappy message like that, Chaka."

"I know that, Gray. But I've got it. The meaning of the J."

"Oh?"

"Juliet."

"Juliet...Juliet!"

☽

We sit around the table as we have many times before. Only now there are no hands to hold but each other's. Mine stretched across to join Chaka's. Hers stretched across the table to join mine.

Together we chant.

"Juliet, the spirit of Juliet, if you are with us give us a sign."

Nothing.

"Juliet, please reveal yourself to those who remember and love you."

Nothing.

"Ya think we're doing this right?" Chaka asks.

"No," I reply. "But I think we'll stumble upon something right."

"Maybe we should call Derderva. He's been around Brenda long enough to have learned a few things."

"No, we can't call him," I tell her. "He told me he was going to see Plotzman this morning with the new evidence. That's important."

"I need coffee," Chaka says.

"Of course you do. Let's get some."

Back in the kitchen the *J* has become an *A*, and now we're sure it's Juliet, because after all, her ghost always went by the name Artemis. How had we forgotten?

We are sipping Taster's Choice instant because nobody bothered to keep the house stocked with freshly ground beans. That's okay. Coffee is coffee, even if it is laced with every chemical known to freeze-dry the brain of mankind. We are back at the table. Holding hands, except when we sip.

"Artemis, please come and have your say," I chant, looking upward. Most of the spirits have come from that direction.

"Oh, please, Artemis, please," Chaka begs. "There's a reason for the lemons, isn't there?"

A door slams.

She's here.

I hope she's not angry. She never used to slam doors while attending to her housekeeping duties.

Now, it seems, we hear the sounds very specific to a life of housekeeping cut short.

Water goes on. Water goes off. A toilet flushes. Twice. A broom sails through the room. Unoccupied. It's like Mary Poppins with PMS.

A fire starts in the fireplace. I am not kidding. My fingers begin to tingle.

The broom joins the flames and burns, exhaling new breaths of fire, a new combustion of heat and fuel, popping with delight as it crackles to nothing.

A woman cries out. She is laughing like a hyena, then segues to sobs, a smooth transition to hysteria.

It is her.

"We miss you, Artemis."

"And I, my lovely children, miss you too," she says from the hollows of the fireplace; her voice, obviously, the source of the blaze. "You have grown to be such beautiful, beautiful people. How I've missed out!"

"Artemis, the lemons?" Chaka asks, not allowing the poor woman even one moment of melancholy.

"Mine."

"The *A*? The *J*?"

"Mine. Mine too."

"What brings you back here?"

"It's so urgent, children. I have a message from your father."

"Father!"

"Father!"

"He says to keep on probing. You're not very far."

"We've been waiting to hear from him," I explain, speaking directly to the fire, making eye contact with an occasional flicker, hoping the spirit will see directly into my soul. "We've been waiting for a sign. So far nothing."

"But I have come," she says, "at a most urgent time."

"What is so urgent?"

"I died a lemon death!"

"What?"

"I died a lemon death!"

"Artemis, please," Chaka says. "You had a heart attack."

"I died a lemon death!"

"What, pray tell, is a lemon death?" I ask.

"He killed me with lemons," she replies.

"Who? Father?" Chaka asks, horrified.

"Of course not."

The flames jump about suddenly, as if a fist has pummeled them from below, as if a stoker may be mixing up the very truth the fire hopes to reveal.

"Who killed you with lemons?" I ask.

"He did."

"So the killer is a man..." Chaka concludes.

"Yes, Chaka," the spirit says.

"But who? Who killed you? What's his name?" I beg.

"He's the same man who killed your father."

Chaka gasps for air.

So do I.

"Yikes," I say. "*Really* yikes."

"Then it couldn't be Bobby," Chaka says to the fire. "Because you died before I even knew him."

I look at Chaka. She looks at me. I shrug. She shrugs. I look again to the fire; I think the flames are shrugging as well.

"I cannot confirm or deny that, Norma Lee," our dead housekeeper says.

Chaka begins to weep. "You must be near Father. He loved that name, 'Norma Lee.' Wasn't so crazy about 'Chaka.' "

"A wise man," I say softly.

"Now don't go judging people for taking on new identities," Artemis/Juliet warns me.

I feel reprimanded and bow my head in remorse. "I'm sorry," I tell the spirit. "Really, I am. But this all would be so much easier if Father would just come forward and reveal himself to us."

"He will, children, he will. Once you have found the killer, you will hear from your father. He can't wait to speak to you. He is so proud of you both."

"Are we on the right track?" I ask.

"As I've said, you're not far."

"But," I persist, hating to mince words with a ghost, but doing it anyway, "are we not far from the killer, or not far from the right track to find the killer?"

"I died a lemon death!"

"But..."

"Go! You have a funeral to attend to. A show you must see."

"But Artemis..."

"I died a lemon death!"

The flames collapse. The fireplace is tauntingly empty. There is a dead hole now where only moments ago there had been a voice and a spirit. I smelled her familiar scent. I reveled in her familiar voice. Somehow Juliet, our housekeeper from way back when, must have suffered a heart attack by means of a dangerous lemon.

We have a funeral to arrange.

And a show to attend.

Twenty-Six

On a bluff overlooking the choppy ocean that encircles Martha's Vineyard, Brenda Cloudholder will rest her skin and bones. But I believe her spirit, her soul, her unblinded vision has already made the initial climb to heaven.

We recite the Lord's Prayer.

Derderva holds a recalcitrant Lourdes, who purrs the purr of a feline numbed by a loved one's death. The wind whispers a few nothings in my ear. Is it the voice of Artemis? Of Grandmother? No, I realize they have stayed away, perhaps so as not to upstage this important farewell. It is only the wind.

I read a verse of Walt Whitman.

Chaka sings "Swing Low, Sweet Chariot."

I never knew my sister could sing. She attributes her vocal ability to training with the Solid Rock Church of God gospel choir. And all along I thought she was only hemming their gowns.

Derderva, sobbing sweetly, servant to the very end, tosses handfuls of dirt onto the casket. He rises from the ground now, his hand to his mouth, holding in the sheer volume of his torment. That, or hiccups. I'm not sure.

Reverend Something or Other makes kind remarks about Brenda. Lourdes sniffles. Then she dives from Derderva's arms and leaps into mine.

Derderva is horrified.

I am amused.

Undaunted by the gray chill of early winter, seagulls swoop in formation over the burial site.

Brenda used to feed the gulls. I remember that.

The gulls fly several passes overhead like military jets in final salute to a fallen comrade.

One shits, and—swear to God—the whitish goop lands smack-dab on Derderva's head. It's a good thing he's wearing a hat, though I do believe the shit has to land on one's exposed head for one to be blessed with the legendary good luck promised by such a bird offering. I don't think it counts if you're wearing a hat.

Chaka roars.

I try not to, but I can't help it. The gull crap is sitting atop Derderva's cap like marshmallow on an ice cream sundae. Reverend Something or Other pretends not to notice, but I see amusement in his brightened eyes, restraint at the corners of his mouth.

"It's not funny," Derderva says.

"No, of course not," I agree.

"Then why are you laughing?"

Chaka walks over to him, eyeing the bird shit cautiously, and puts an arm around his shoulders. "It's okay, Derderva. Maybe this is Brenda's way of giving us a good laugh in a time of sorrow."

"Maybe," he mutters. "But I need a new hat."

"I'm sure we can dig one up at the house."

He is startled. "Brenda's house?"

"No, I was thinking we must have some spare hats at Sea Valley," Chaka assures him.

"Because we can't go to Brenda's house," he says.

"Is there a problem?" I ask.

"No," he replies. "No problem. I just want to preserve the house exactly as Brenda left it. You understand?"

"Indeed," I tell him. "You're thinking of building a shrine to her."

"Maybe."

"Oh, Derderva, how wonderful," my sister says, giving him a squeeze, pecking his cheek. "Brenda would be so proud."

His eyes fill.

The gulls squawk loudly.

Bird shit drying on his hat, Derderva turns away and follows a lonely path to the waiting Yugo.

☽

I first notice the waiting cruiser after I press "end" on my cell phone. I've just called a cab.

"Look," I say.

Chaka looks.

"The cops," I say.

"Hmm."

I'm wrong. It's not *the* cops. It is *a* cop. A lone officer is sitting in a cruiser watching the two of us as we make our way closer. A window rolls down. The profile turns and becomes a face. The face of Detective Plotzman.

"Good morning," he says.

"Morning."

"I'm sorry to hear about your friend," he tells us.

My sister thanks him for the sentiment. "We are so sorry to lose her," she says.

"Yes, I'm sure. Do you two have a minute?"

"Well, I've called for a cab."

The detective snorts a hearty New England snort and says, "Well, in that case you have a few hours!"

"What can we do for you?" I ask.

"Well, Ms. Cloudholder's chauffeur came to see me yesterday with information that we need to talk about."

"Bobby Bose?"

"Exactly."

The detective swings open the door and makes a jaws-of-life effort to extricate his bulbous flesh from the car. I want to tell him that the murderer could not possibly be Bobby Bose, given what we've learned from Juliet, but I have yet to figure out a way to explain that my source of information is the dearly departed. But truly I'd be surprised if Plotzman were surprised. After all, everyone on the island knows that Brenda Cloudholder had been spending lots of time with the Hoffenstein children lately, and everyone knows she wasn't teaching us how to bake pie.

"Does the evidence hold up?" I ask the portly officer.

"I'm not sure it's evidence," he says. I'm relieved (I think). "I'll need your help."

"Today?"

"The sooner the better."

"It can't be today," I tell him. "We have to make a flight back to Boston."

My sister narrows her eyes at me and wrinkles her forehead, and I flash her a look, begging her with my eyes to cooperate. We must not help the detective bring in Bobby Bose if Bobby Bose is the wrong man. We must find the right man. I have never been so sure of anything in my life (except for my revelations about gay men and moisturizers, the Bionic Woman, black people and children, and a more recent conclusion that the grass is always greener in someone else's life, so to thine own fertilizer be true).

"Could you spend another night on the island?"

Confidently, Chaka shakes her head no. "You don't understand," she says. "Gray's boyfriend, Pedro, is performing in his first drag show tonight. We have to be there."

I step ever so lightly (maybe not so lightly) on Chaka's foot. "That is not going to help our case," I whisper between my clenched teeth.

She ignores me. "He's doing Charo," she yelps, as if dropping the name of a famous-for-being-famous bosomy blond lends any credibility whatsoever to our plight.

"Damsels?" the detective asks.

My eyes follow my chin and drop to the ground. My sister is first to slice the stunning silence, asking, "You know Damsels?"

"As a matter of fact, I do."

"In what capacity, Detective?" she continues to probe. "Audience or...cast member?"

We all get a good laugh out of that. A good, quick laugh because the detective turns serious again. "Neither," he says. "We used to get a lot of the old drag queens retiring to the island. Don't know why."

"Maybe they felt protected and anonymous here," Chaka says.

Plotzman shrugs. "Don't know. I do know one of them was quite the dead ringer for Bernadette Peters."

Folding my arms across my chest, I say, "I always thought Bernadette Peters was a drag queen trapped in a woman's body."

The remark soars over the detective's head; the expression in its wake is a blank stare, then a shift of the eyes and a shift of his very, very, very big hips. "Why didn't you two come forward about this earlier?" he asks.

"Forward about what?"

"Bobby Bose."

I look at Chaka. She looks at me. He looks at both of us. "Well?"

"We just aren't convinced it's true," my sister answers.

"Not even if there's a means, a motive, and an opportunity?" the detective asks.

"I don't know," Chaka says. "I just don't know. Bobby has done some stupid things with his life, but murder—I don't think he has it in him."

"I'm not so sure," I say.

"But you still believe it wasn't your mother?"

"Absolutely," I reply.

"Absolutely," Chaka repeats. Then, "Really, Detective, we have a flight to catch."

"Forget the cab," the detective tells us. "I'll give you a lift."

"We have to stop at *Entr*—Sea Valley for our things," I explain.

"No problem," he tells us. "Get in."

We get in. The door locks automatically. We're in the backseat with no way out, not unlike criminals being hauled off to headquarters. I hate feeling like a criminal; it unleashes the paranoid feelings I have occasionally of being accused of something like murder or bank robbery or smoking at the gas pump when I absolutely did not commit the crime—but no one believes me and no one comes to my defense and the state won't even provide me a lawyer! Crazy, I know.

"Do you have any African-American officers on the police force?" Chaka asks through the slices of metal grate separating the front seat from the back.

"One."

"Just one?"

"It's representative of the island's population," Plotzman says unapologetically.

"With the rich black heritage of Oak Bluffs?" my sister argues.

"Just one."

"Oh," my sister says tentatively.

I roll my eyes.

"Do you believe in affirmative action?" my sister asks.

I nudge my elbow into her and give her a wicked, jaw-clenched look. My eyes are narrow. Very narrow. I can barely see.

"Never mind," she tells Plotzman.

"You know, Detective," I say, "if I thought we could free Mother tonight, I'd gladly forgo the show at Damsels and stay."

"Of course you would."

"But we can't. Can we? We couldn't get Mother out of jail tonight, could we?"

"I'm afraid not," Plotzman replies. "In fact, I'm not sure that's ever an option. Ever."

"Ever?" my sister says with a nervous twitter in her voice.

"I'm afraid so. It takes a lot to undo an investigation, folks. That's why I need your help eliminating Bobby Bose as a serious suspect."

"You want our help to eliminate Bobby?" I ask incredulously. "So you can keep Mother right where she is, locked up in some rape factory of a jail!"

"I wouldn't put it that way."

"Then how would you put it, Detective?" I persist. "The sooner you can dismiss Bobby Bose as a suspect, the sooner you can put the case back in some dented file cabinet in your pathetic little office."

"Mr. Hoffenstein, really..."

"Don't *really* me!" I cry. "How dare you turn this around, Detective! We're trying to clear our mother's name and you know that." I want to pound his fat face with the hammer Ginkie the cook had used so many times to pound Father's favorite cuts of veal. "But all you're doing is trying to keep her in jail...all you're doing is covering your fat ugly ass so you won't look bad for putting the wrong person behind bars. Stop the car!"

"Gray," Chaka whispers.

"Stop the damn car!"

The car stops.

I can't get out.

"Unlock the door, Detective."

He steps out of the cruiser and opens the door on Chaka's side. She doesn't move. He then approaches my side and opens that door. I scoot out, grabbing my sister by the arm and pulling her across the squeaky vinyl seat.

"We'll walk from here," I announce.

"As you wish," the detective says, undaunted, it seems, by the very defiant offspring of very rich people. He has seen wealthy tantrums on the island many, many times before, I imagine. Nothing fazes him. Not even drag queens.

He drives away.

"Walk, my ass," Chaka declares, reaching for my cell phone.

She dials. And we wait for a cab.

Twenty-Seven

Madame Jenufleck has the scarred voice of a gambler, a woman who has smoked too many cigarettes between her pulls at slots. She is about as old as a gambling woman, I imagine. Fifty-eight, maybe sixty. It's hard to say. Lights flood her with tacky Vegas colors, making an ordinary gown shimmer, wave, and swirl.

Her hair is piled atop her head, filtering light from behind. Dazzling, really.

She is telling us about the show.

We clap.

She throws a few jabs at us (she insults the size of our penises—as if we all share one, she calls us whores, she declares this the Year of the Yeast Infection). She's in charge. This is her show. Her glamour, her wisecracking repertoire, her dance with stardom.

She's been doing this for years.

I'm not guessing that. It's what she says. She tells us she owns more shoes than Imelda Marcos. I think that joke is rather tired.

But we laugh.

Music takes over.

Celebrated music that audiences drool for.

"Once again, welcome to Damsels. Sit back and enjoy the show. And keep your hands to yourself!" With that, Madame Jenufleck grabs what's left of her crotch (tucked away all these years by professional necessity somewhere in her layers of undergarment) and gives us a saucy wink.

The room blacks out, soaking the audience in anticipation.

And then, moments later, seven beauties appear in sequins and jewels and hair, hair, hair.

Their faces are old and young, but it's not the faces that reveal their ages. It's their necks and their creases and folds and purse-like sags, or lack thereof, that separate the men from the boys, or the women from the girls, or whatever you call the performer in performance.

Is he a she only when he/she performs?

Or is he always/never a she?

Sometimes a she? Sometimes a he?

Regardless of performance?

Chaka elbows me. "You don't look like you're enjoying yourself."

I say nothing.

Stevie puts his hand on my shoulder. "I know this is hard for you, Gray."

"It's not that hard," I say. "I'm just trying to get a handle on the whole thing."

Skye smiles her sweet, expensive smile and says, "Gray, you think too much. There's too much Jewish in you."

I smile. Maybe that's true.

I'm bracing myself for Pedro, for his lipstick, his eye shadow, his high heels, his breasts.

"It's amazing," Chaka says. "You'd never know it's him."

"Who?"

"Pedro."

"Where?"

"C'mon, Gray, on stage," she replies.

I look. I look hard.

No. Can't be.

"Which one?"

"That one," Stevie says, pointing to the second one on the left, the one that looks like Charo.

It's Pedro. One of the seven beauties.

He is beautiful.

Have I never noticed the softness of his skin? The chandelier sparkle of his eyes? Have I never noticed the width of his smile and how it makes you feel like you're at the center of the world, in the heart of a satisfied ocean, in the arms of God?

Skye orders a drink. Perrier with lime.

The waiter says they have Pellegrino, not Perrier. Skye says "whatever" or "who cares" and dismisses him with her eyes.

Stevie gives her a loving squeeze.

Chaka isn't wearing a bra.

Six beauties leave the stage. One remains.

"And now ladies and gentlemen, and gentlemen who prefer to be ladies, Damsels presents an international pageant of stars. Please give a warm welcome to Miss Diamond Bubbles!"

Come on.

A spotlight comes up on Diamond Bubbles and we clap.

We hear the typical songs of Barbra Streisand. "People." "The Way We Were." "Evergreen."

(Love, mind you, is not soft as an easy chair. It's more like a menstrual cramp.)

Lawrence Welk bubbles pour from the ceiling; we are won over. Diamond takes a graceful bow and throws the audiences many kisses.

I have to pee. But I'm reluctant to leave lest Pedro take the stage and I miss his performance. We're sitting at the very end of the stage's runway, around a small circular cocktail table. I survey the four exit signs, beneath one a sign for the rest rooms. My bladder is screaming. I decide to make a go for it.

I have two choices, a door marked DAMSELS and another marked THE REST OF YOU. I choose the latter and piss my brains out.

I listen for the sounds of Charo and hear none. On the way back to the table I quickly study a hallway of 8-by-10s, photos of past and present drag queens who have taken to this hallowed stage, who have belted out Liza numbers, wisecracked like Bette, melted audiences with ballads, crooned love songs, stuffed and padded and teased and pancaked themselves into a stupor.

"And now, ladies and gentlemen, before we break for intermission, let us present, in her international debut, Carmen Cuernavaca bringing you the very best of Charo!"

The very best? Is there anything more than *cootchie cootchie*?

Rousing applause. Latin is very *in.*

Pedro.

Beautiful. It's frightening. I'm so proud of him suddenly. So impressed. He can do drag all he wants. But must he cut it off? Must he make such a drastic move? Maybe he doesn't really want to be a woman. Maybe he just wants to accessorize. And that's fine. Isn't it?

Oh, my head is sinking into the deep, sorrowful graveyard of my psyche. My eyes fill up. I see Stevie watching me. I see compassion in his eyes. He knows I need a little sympathy. Pedro is telling some jokes, an intense Spanish accent in his voice. The audience is roaring, but I have no idea what he is saying. I can only stare (the volume turned off, his lips moving tragically) at my past, at the present, watching the future slipping out of my hands, not unlike a widow witnessing her husband's casket sinking into the ground. This is death, it is murder, call it what you will. It is the end. And I am desperately sad.

Guantanamera.

The music is coming out of Pedro's mouth like manic birdsong on a bright Mexican morning. *Guantanamera.*

The audience leaps to its feet.

Stevie drags me to mine.

Pedro throws me a kiss. I wipe my eyes and touch my hand to my lips, blowing a kiss back at him. "Dear Pedro," I say softly amidst the rousing applause, "goodbye to you. It was fun while it lasted."

❩

They see my tear-stained face and agree to take me home.

"I'm so sorry, Gray," Skye tells me. "You really love him, don't you?"

"I do."

"Let me go pay the tab," Stevie says. "Then we can get out of here."

"Nothing like having your divorce played out for you in front of two hundred people," Chaka says ruefully. "It's like the opposite of a wedding."

"Kind of," I confess.

Stevie returns. He has paid the tab and retrieved our coats from the cloakroom. He has been followed.

"Sneaking out during intermission?"

It's Madame Jenufleck.

We laugh, playing along, ready to take the barbs, the bitchy, catty remarks about our hair, clothes, body parts, most recent orgasms.

"We have a plane to catch," I lie.

"Oh...my...goddess!" the hostess cries. "Look who we have here!" She clutches her chest, feigning cardiac arrest, then a hand goes to her brow. "First you sneak in, then you sneak out! Why didn't you tell us you were here, doll face? Why didn't you tell us you were back?"

She is speaking to Skye, whose only response is a bemused, bewildered, frightened stare (deer sees headlights, deer doesn't understand headlights, deer realizes it's too late).

"Stand up and let me look at you, you old bitch," Madame Jenufleck demands.

We are silent and still. We don't want a scene. Although it is clearly too late to not want a scene considering that this, indeed, is a scene, and we are stuck. We don't want to offend the woman; she is the hostess, the master of ceremonies, so to speak. She is in charge, but she has obviously mistaken Skye for somebody else.

Madame Jenufleck grabs Skye by the hand and pulls her to her feet. Skye feigns a laugh and the drag queen hoists my sister's face to her bosom and holds it there, squeezing and pushing.

"I don't think she can breathe," I say.

"Hush now," Madame Jenufleck tells me. "We haven't seen Bionica in more than a year. Don't spoil the moment."

"Bionica?" Stevie asks. "I think you've got the wrong girl."

Madame Jenufleck crackles with laughter. "Well, aren't you the protective little lily licker! No one knows her real name, stupid. But she's Bionica to us. And we'd given her up for dead!"

Skye breaks free from the drag queen's breasts.

"One of the doormen recognized you, sweetheart, and started spreading the word you were in the house," Madame Jenufleck persists. "Backstage is all abuzz. You must come and let me show you off. You look ravenous. Like you took twenty years off. I knew when you disappeared you made off for some spa somewhere. That's it, isn't it? A little nip, a little tuck?"

"Madame, really, I have no idea what you're talking about," my sister begs. "I've never been here before in my life, never seen you before, never even heard of this place."

"You see?" Stevie asks the hostess.

The woman looks to the floor. She realizes, perhaps, that she has made a dreadful mistake. Her lips are trembling. "I am so sorry, Bionica. I didn't realize nobody knew."

"Knew what, for chrissake?" Chaka asks.

"About Bionica Pie," the woman replies, "one of our most famous drag queens."

I shake my head. "You've been doing drag all these years, Skye, and telling us you're a model?"

Her eyes are disgusted with me. "Right, Gray, and I've been your brother all these years posing as your sister. You're an idiot."

I'm an idiot. Of course I am. My poor sister. Just when she's gaining confidence in herself as a model, someone mistakes her for an old drag queen. The world is crueler to some than others. "Look," I tell the hostess, "we're really sorry to disappoint you, but my sister, though she may look like a drag queen, is not your Bionica Thigh."

"Pie," she corrects me.

"Whoever."

Stevie holds Skye by the hand protectively, but I see doubt about her in his eyes. When someone calls your girlfriend a drag queen (by the name of Bionica Pie, no less), it must be a bit unsettling. He is doing his best. He is the greatest.

Chaka throws her fur around her shoulders. It looks like a cape. Her unharnessed breasts are huge now that she is several months into her pregnancy, and they are sticking out from the draped fur, her textured nipples pressing against her blouse like platters of neatly arranged fruit.

I zip up my leather parka.

The woman grabs a flashlight from a passing usher and holds it up, illuminating Skye's face. She studies my sister under this nakedly revealing light and is suddenly mystified, mesmerized, and ultimately, horrified. She brings her hand to her forehead as though she might faint; she wipes her brow. "I am so sorry! I don't know what to say. What an embarrassment!"

"I'm not your Bionica Pie?" Skye asks.

"Heavens, no," Madame Jenufleck replies. "You're much too young. You're every bit as beautiful, sweetheart, but Bionica was old enough to be your mother."

We laugh. We are relieved.

"Please let me make this awful mistake up to you, please," the hostess begs. "Stay for the next act. Drinks are on me. As much as you'd like."

I shake my head. "No. Thank you," I tell her. "We came to see my boyfriend perform. And his act is over."

"Your boyfriend?"

"Charo."

"Magnificent."

"Thank you."

We head for the lobby.

"Wait," she calls to us. "I want you to see an old photo of Bionica. One look at it and you'll see the striking resemblance. I promise."

"No, really, that's okay," Skye tells her.

"Please, I insist," the woman says.

Chaka snorts. "Jesus Christ, all right, already, get the damn picture. I have to pee anyway."

She excuses herself to the bathroom, where I presume she pees.

She returns before Madame Jenufleck does, and we are standing there, the four of us, waiting and shaking our heads at what has become a confusing and disturbing evening. Then I hear the swift and urgent *click-clack* of Madame Jenufleck's heels. I look up. The woman is racing toward us, rushing us, a photograph dangling from her spiky red fingernails.

She is out of breath.

"It used to hang in the hallway with the rest of our stars," she pants. "See? Can you see the resemblance?"

Can we ever.

Our circle of eyes stare at the photograph understanding, in silent unison, everything and nothing at all. It's a glossy head shot of Father.

In drag.

Twenty-Eight

"Father was a drag queen!"

I can think of less conspicuous things to shout out in a crowded theater. "Fire!" for example. Undaunted, Chaka repeats herself.

"Father was a drag queen!"

"It would appear that way, yes," I say.

Madame Jenufleck, meanwhile, is frozen still, her hand to her mouth.

"Tell us it isn't so," Skye pleads.

The gowned drag queen moves her eyes from left to right as if they're doing as much listening as her ears. She studies Skye and smiles. "I'm afraid it is. I guess I created one big mess for all of you."

"Seems like there was a side of him we didn't know," I say.

"You're telling me!" Skye concurs.

"Ahh, just look at you, my dear," Madame Jenufleck says to my baby sister, touching her hand to Skye's Oil of Olay skin, "you are your father's daughter. Surely now you can understand my confusion, can't you?"

Skye eyes her doubtfully but says nothing.

"Dear, it makes perfect sense that your father in drag would look like...well...might just look like one of his very own daughters."

"Really?" Skye asks wistfully. Beautiful and sweet, yes, but my baby sister is no tornado of intelligence.

"Of course," I tell her. "You're his flesh and blood. You

have his eyes. His nose. The bone structure. Put a little make-up on, take thirty years off, and Father might have had a modeling career as promising as yours."

"Stop!" she cries. "I can't bear it." Of course she can't. Only hours ago she returned from the Massachusetts Correctional Institute at Framingham where, for the first time, she visited with Mother. She came home sobbing, unable to reconcile the sight of Mother behind bars. The poor girl was traumatized. And now this. It's like her inner child has been spanked by both parents.

Stevie pulls her close. She rests her face against his comforting chest.

I raise my eyebrows and launch a hard stare at Madame Jenufleck. "I think you have some explaining to do."

"Of course," she says. "Follow me backstage."

We do.

It is a jungle of costumes and jewelry back here, lingerie, feather boas, and wigs, wigs, wigs. Two drag queens are chatting up a storm calling each other "girlfriend" and reapplying eyeliner, lipstick, and in some cases, retucking their private parts rather publicly. You know in an instant that there is no shame back here. Of course there's no shame, given the line of work, given the guts it takes for a man to be a woman. Now, that's macho.

The men have affected womanly voices; I'm sure some of them speak as deeply as Clint Eastwood or John Wayne during their nine-to-five lives as teachers, bus drivers, pastry chefs, and police officers, but here they let go of their defenses, revel in abandon, throw their heads back, laugh wildly, and shave their armpits.

They look less like women and more like mental patients when they're wigless. It's just that look: all made up, exaggerated colors around their eyes, blush-stained cheeks, oozing lips, no hair.

"We never saw your father as a man," Madam Jenufleck

tells us, leading us through a doorway from the dressing area to a separate room, a business office, perhaps. "Sit," she says.

We comply. Chaka, Skye, and Stevie stay close, side-by-side on a velour divan. I take a seat in an office chair opposite the drag queen.

"Was Father homosexual?" Chaka asks.

"No," Madame Jenufleck replies. "Absolutely not. We didn't know much about him. But we knew he wasn't gay. All the men were dying to be with him. But he never, ever accepted their advances."

"Then what the hell was he doing here?" Chaka asks the woman.

"He was an actor, a performer. And everyone loved him. He was *so* good," Madame Jenufleck says nostalgically as her eyes lovingly embrace the photograph of Father. She is holding it in her lap. There is no doubt about it; it is him. But I have to keep staring at the picture to be sure. Even when I'm sure I'm sure, I still have to be even more sure. "He told us very little about his life, and we didn't ask," she continues. "You know—don't ask, don't tell. And it was quite a feat, let me tell you. After all, he performed here for more than five years."

"Five years," Chaka repeats.

"I wonder if Mother knew," Skye says.

Chaka laughs. "Of course not. If Mother knew, there would have been a divorce."

"Not necessarily," I say.

"I promise you, Gray," Chaka retorts, "Mother didn't know. All she knew was he was always flying off to every foreign country on the map and never coming home with any deals. That would make her so angry. He'd be gone for days, sometimes weeks at a time, and come home empty-handed. Don't you remember those fights?"

No one answers.

Chaka continues. "Obviously, Father never stepped out of

the damn country. Instead he was stepping out on the stage getting whatever jollies he got from wearing women's underwear." She shakes her head. "Lord ha' mercy!"

"For whatever it's worth, Chaka, I don't this think has anything to do with women's underwear," I say. "I can ask Pedro, but I think the performers here probably wear their own underwear onstage. I mean, I think there's a difference between being a drag queen—a performer, if you will—and a transvestite."

Madame Jenufleck interjects. "I think what your brother is saying is that, for most of our performers, this isn't just about putting on women's clothes. This is an art."

"Hmph!" Chaka snorts.

Stevie laughs.

I don't know why.

I suppose he is the only one left who can see the insanity for what it is.

"Oh, no," Skye whispers.

"What is it?" Stevie asks her.

"Oh, no," she repeats. "Maybe Mother *did* kill him."

I stare at her, begging for more. "What?"

"My God, Gray, Mother has never *denied* they were arguing," Skye says. "That much came out in the trial. And now I understand what they were arguing about."

"Please, Nancy Drew, do tell us..."

"Cele found out what Father was up to," my younger sister explains. "She found out about all this...all this cross-dressing. Somebody probably recognized Father in costume and told Mother. Rather than face public humiliation from here to Saint-Tropez, she killed him."

I stand up. "You're dead wrong, Skye! Dead wrong! Do you honestly believe Mother is capable of murder?" No one answers. I begin to panic. The walls shift, the floor spins, the ceiling blurs and hazes. I grip the back of the chair in my hands. "C'mon, someone say something," I beg.

"I'm stunned," Madame Jenufleck says softly. She is shaking her head back and forth, not knowing where to look. She's searching the room, perhaps for the truth. "You mean Bionica Pie is dead? Bionica Pie was murdered?"

"Call him what you want," Chaka tells her. "Colin Lightfoot Hoffenstein was murdered."

The drag queen gasps. Then sobs. She heaves scarred spasms of misery and woe from her throat and turns to the mirror. She watches her makeup run down her face, streams of it rushing through the dry cake of her facial grooves like a flash flood through a desert wash. She reaches for tissues and pulls them from their dispenser with a flourish.

"Yes, but Mother didn't have anything to do with the murder," I say, feeling less faint.

"I'm telling you," Skye insists, "she found out what Father was up to all those years. And she freaked. She just went wild. I mean, you've described the scene many times, Gray. She threw a glass of wine at him. Who knows what really happened next?"

"Shut up, Skye," Chaka says. "You're upsetting Gray."

"But—"

"Chaka's right, Skye," Stevie tells her.

"Whose side are you on, anyway?" she asks him.

He pecks her cheek but doesn't answer. I know deep in my heart that Stevie Goldman is on my side. He may be fucking my sister, but he's on my side. Always will be.

"Your mother didn't kill Bionica Pie," Madame Jenufleck announces from her mirror. She doesn't look at us, but rather studies her reflection, or something behind it, way back on the other side of the mirror, history maybe, as she talks to us amid falling tears. "If only I had taken Mona more seriously..."

"Mona?" I ask.

"Mona Kahona," she replies.

"Of course, *that* Mona..." is all I can say.

"Bionica Pie just disappeared...I never knew there had

been a murder. If I had known Bionica was dead, I could have led the police right to her killer."

"What are you saying?" I beg, almost in tears myself, stricken with grief all over again, the same way I was when I first heard the words "Father is dead."

"I mean, it's very simple," the drag queen says, removing herself from the crystal distance of the looking glass and turning to her audience. "If Bionica Pie is dead, if your father is dead, I know who killed both of them."

"Both of them?" Skye asks, clearly trying to do the math in her head.

I shush her.

Chaka lunges for the drag queen and pulls her from her chair. She grabs the woman's necklace and says, "Spill it, honey."

"Oh, dear, be gentle. My heart is so weak tonight."

Chaka apologizes. "We're very nerved up about this. You can understand."

The drag queen nods and returns to her chair, needlessly straightening up things on her dressing table, nervously arranging jewelry. "Well, Bionica Pie disappeared a year ago September."

September. A year ago. Same time as Father's murder. The room is cold. My skin is clammy. A chill grips the back of my neck, tingles at my ears.

"She finished her show. And never came back."

"You didn't recognize my father's picture all over the newspapers and TV when he was murdered?" Chaka asked.

"Your father came and left as Bionica Pie. Like I said, we never saw him as a man. Never knew what he really looked like. And, no, I don't think I would have made any connection with your father's murder. I'm not even sure I was aware of it."

"Had something gone wrong for Bionic...er...Father?" I ask.

"Terribly," I am told by the tear-streaked woman. "She had gone up against the wrong lady. Mona Kahona was as vindictive a drag queen as there ever was. Performed here ever since she was a kid, practically. Been here some twenty-five years—an institution, if you ask me—and along comes Bionica Pie about five years ago and starts stirring things up. Bionica has better costumes, better songs, better jokes, and as God is my witness, is drawing bigger crowds. The biggest we had had in years."

"Mona was jealous," I conclude.

" 'Jealous' is a very sweet, darling way of putting it," I am told. "She was enveloped by envy, overcome by it, completely consumed. It led to many catfights back here. Mona starting stealing Bionica's accessories...and you could tell this was not costume jewelry, this was the real stuff. No one knew where Bionica got the money for all her jewels and gowns, but everyone knew Mona was out to get Bionica any way she could. The last time any of us saw Bionica Pie was one night after a show...." She pauses. Her eyes dart from side to side as if collecting data from the images of her memory. "Yes," the hostess continues, "after the finale, the girls were undressing and we all heard screaming coming from the alley outside the stage door... Being a bunch of curious pussyqueens, we, of course, all dash outside to see what's going on. And it was a catfight to end all catfights! Bionica had finally confronted Mona about the stealing, and Mona just about blew an ovary. Oh, heavens, Mona was out there pulling at Bionica's hair, ripping at her gown, kicking her shins. Poor Bionica was trying to be a lady and talk things out, but Mona would have none of that. It was a fur-flying fiasco until a few of us jumped in and pulled Mona off your father. Your father limped down the alley and out of our lives, Mona all the while calling to him, 'If I lay eyes on you again, I'll be the last one to do so! You're a dead kitten!' Of course, no one really took the threat seriously. Drag queens get a little bitchy now and then."

She stares at us as if we fully understand. We stare back at her, a mosaic of mystified faces.

"It's like PMS with a penis," she explains. "Anyway, we never saw Bionica again. Ever. Mona did a few more shows that week. And then she too disappeared."

"Wow!" I say.

"I don't believe it," Chaka gasps. But she does believe it. I can tell her disbelief is nothing more than a form of speech, a dramatic way to predicate a dramatic story.

"Yikes," Stevie says. "Yikes and then some."

Madame Jenufleck shakes her head. "This is a dirty business. The world of female impersonators is full of huge egos, too many divas, and backstabbing galore. To think their two photos used to hang side by side in our front hallway."

"They were friends at one time?" I ask.

"For a very short time. When Bionica first arrived here, Mona took her under her wing. Showed her around. Taught her the do's and don'ts. They spent a lot of time together that first year. And then we gave Bionica Pie top billing. And that was it! The friendship was over faster than you can say 'Go fish!' "

"You say their pictures hung side by side?" Stevie asks with the inflection of a lawyer on cross-examination.

"Yes. Tragic, isn't it?" she replies.

"And Mona's picture is where?" Stevie inquires.

She hesitates. "Well, probably the same place I found Bionica's."

"Which is?"

"That closet," Madame Jenufleck answers, pointing to a door across the room.

"Please," Stevie urges her, "if you can dig it out, I'm sure we all would like to see."

She complies, heading for the closet, shedding her grief, it seems, with this new mission.

We hear her rummaging through boxes and piles of papers, restacking things on shelves.

She returns, a photo in hand.

She offers it to Stevie, who simply shrugs and shakes his head, then passes it to me.

Chaka circles around me and studies the black-and-white glossy from behind my shoulder. I can sense the nod of her head behind me. The recognition we share. Together we stare at the image, soaking in the face that is familiar to both of us. It is a person we have come to know so well over these past few months. A person who has made a life serving others.

This photograph also explains the dancer in flowing chiffon and lace in the backyard of Brenda Cloudholder's home.

It is a person who drives a Yugo.

It is Derderva.

Twenty-Nine

Detective Plotzman looks at me like I have a few too many heads, eyes dangling from my sockets, a 747-size wart on my nose.

"Really," I assure him, "we know what we're doing."

He laughs loudly. "You're crazy," he tells me. "But if this makes you happy."

"It makes me very happy, Detective. I'm overjoyed."

The man may be laughing, but he is terrified. Terrified and apprehensive, and I am not without sympathy. I can understand how we look to him, especially now at three o'clock in the morning; I am here with Stevie and Skye and Chaka and, yes, Pedro, whom we swiped from backstage at Damsels before he had a chance to un-Charo himself. We piled into a cab, piled out of it at Logan Airport, and rented a plane.

With Stevie at the controls, we flew through the purple sky, the night pregnant with tremendous possibilities. Leaning up against the fuselage, where the vibrations met my ear with all the glory of a musical overture, I listened to the hum and roar of the propeller engines. Something magnificent was only a tailwind away. Pedro fell asleep on my shoulder. I told him I loved him, and told him again in Spanish.

Te amo. Te amo mucho.

The moon followed us. Beaming in the windows of the small airplane. In the moon's glow, Skye became a new woman, her translucent skin suggesting the richness of life and meaning residing now in her soul. Her eyes looked older, wiser, so much less tentative. She is in on this. She was meant to be. I love her for letting herself be a conduit of truth.

Chaka threw up twice during the flight. We were flying low enough to heave the vomit-filled bag out the window. Most likely, it landed in the ocean. Or perhaps on a Cape Cod cottage. We were nowhere near Hyannisport, so the Kennedy compound was spared.

And so it was that this odd concoction of friends and lovers, sisters and brothers shuffled up the front walk to Detective Plotzman's weather-beaten saltbox home. Its shingles were perfect imperfection. Bathed in the same moonlight that guided us here, the house was inviting. Not so its resident. I rapped on the door several times before hearing heavy, unsteady movement from inside.

"What the hell!" the detective bellowed as he stretched himself awake. He kept the door half-closed between us. I would have too.

"Sorry to get you up at this hour, Detective. But there's a major break in the case," I told him.

"What case?"

I cocked my head. "Why, the murder case of Colin Lightfoot Hoffenstein, of course."

He stuck his fleshy face through the crack in the door. "You have got to be kidding."

"No," I told him. "I'm not. It's Derderva. He killed Father."

"Oh, Jesus," Plotzman growled.

And that's when I asked the portly, partially dressed detective to put all his earthly beliefs, experiences, and predispositions aside and please join us at *Entre Tetas* for a séance.

☽

Somehow I convince him that I have only one head, that my eyes have not sprung from their sockets, that the blemish he notices is not a 747-size wart but, rather, a pimple that had made an emergency landing on my nose on its way to a more adolescent face. Besides, he confesses that Derderva has irked him for some time now, ever since he discovered the Yugo-driving chauffeur moonlighting as a drag queen in Boston.

"You're kidding!" I cry. "You knew about that?"

"Yes. But I found out a long time ago...long before your father's death. There would have been no reason whatsoever to make a connection."

"How?" Skye asks him. "How did you know about Mona Kahona?"

Plotzman chuckles a fat-man chuckle. "Brenda hired me many years ago to do surveillance on Derderva. She had just taken him on as an assistant and wanted him checked out. You know, a background check. I was a new cop on the force and needed the extra money. So I did it in my off time. All I came up with was the drag queen stuff—after following him one night to Boston. Didn't seem to bother Brenda. I think she was amused, in fact. Until he started stealing some of her dresses, you know, the long witchy numbers she used to wear. Well, he'd steal them, then take a sewing machine to them—you know, because he was several sizes smaller than her—and I guess he'd use them in his shows. We confronted him about it very discreetly. He wasn't pleased. He was actually belligerent about it. But then we promised him that it would forever be a secret if he could only find his costumes elsewhere. That seemed to pacify him. And that was the end of it."

"That's it?" Chaka asks as we all ride in the rental car Stevie hot-wired at the airport.

"That's it," Plotzman replies. "Never knew a thing about your father. He probably wanted it that way."

"I should think so," I say. "Did we tell you we had to steal this car?"

"No, I don't think you did."

"Not really *steal*," Skye explains. "We fully intend to pay for it. I mean, it's not like we charter a plane and then don't have the money to pay for a Ford Taurus. But there was no one at the rental counter."

"They tend to go home before three A.M.," Plotzman quips.

"We'll pay them tomorrow," I assure him. "Double."

"Triple," Chaka suggests.

"Quadruple," Stevie tops her.

"*Cootchie cootchie*," my adorable, lovable, cross-dressing boyfriend adds.

We empty out at *Entre Tetas*. We are exhausted but exhilarated. Plotzman still seems tentative. He eyes the front door suspiciously. If it had been any suspect other than Derderva, he probably wouldn't have come. But Derderva struck a nerve.

"So you really use a round table?" the detective asks.

"Of course," Chaka says without inflection.

Doesn't everybody?

Skye lights candles around the room. "What about a fire?" she asks, standing by the large stone hearth.

"It will light itself if it wants to," Chaka tells her.

Satisfied with that answer, Skye joins us at the table. We are all sitting now, except Pedro.

"Honey, can't I please go upstairs to bed?" he asks me. "It's been such a long day."

I shake my head. "I need you here, Pedro. For support."

He acquiesces. And I peck him on his heavily rouged cheek as he sits beside me. The glow of the candles casts enough light for me to see Detective Plotzman roll his eyes at the sight of man kissing man.

I place the picture of Mona Kahona/Derderva at the center of the table. We hold hands. We bow our heads. There is silence but for our breathing, a light wind shimmying at the windows, and the flicker of flame.

"Concentrate," I say.

"Concentrate," Chaka repeats. The word continues to be uttered around the circle.

"Father," I recite, "we have found your killer."

Nothing.

Plotzman glances back and forth, unconvinced, a cynical look in his eyes.

"Father," I repeat, suppressing the desperation I feel in my heart. "You said you'd present yourself when we found your killer. A deal's a deal."

Skye holds up the photo of Mona Kahona. "This look familiar, Father? Or does this?" She pulls the photo of Bionica Pie from beneath the table and waves it high in the air with her other hand.

"Skye..." Stevie says cautiously.

The table rattles.

"Props?" It is Brenda Cloudholder. "Who said you could use props?"

Our grip on one another tightens. The voice of her spirit is coming from the center of the table.

"Is that cheating?" I ask her.

"No, children, it's not cheating," Brenda replies. "The news is shocking."

"It's so good to hear your voice," I tell her.

"Yours too. You all look so wonderful!"

"Look?" Chaka asks. "You can see us?"

"But of course!"

"But you're blind!" I remind her.

"Not anymore," she says playfully. "The soul is never blind."

"Come on, Brenda," Chaka begs, "that's laying it on a bit thick, don't you think?"

"Yes. I suppose it is. Truth is, that bright light when you die, you know, the light at the end of the very long, dark tunnel, it is so fierce, it reversed my blindness. Now I see too well."

"Too well?" I ask.

"High-definition, digital, you name it."

"*Dios mio!*" Pedro cries. "This is too fucking weird."

"Maybe so, lover boy," Brenda says. "But you found *my* killer too."

"*YOUR* KILLER?" I cry.

"What a shock! What a sad, pitiful disappointment of a man," she says.

We hear a chorus of seagulls. A crescendo of squawking fills the room. I am frightened, amazed, overcome. "Derderva killed you?"

"Of course. I was helping you find your father's killer. It was only a matter of time before I led you to Derderva. He had to get me *out of the way,*" she says, as if mocking the cliché that explains her demise.

Plotzman is perspiring heavily. Sweat is pouring from his forehead, and he's beginning to smell.

"How did he do it, Brenda?" Chaka asks the spirit. "How did he kill you?"

"I died a lemon death," she replies.

I gasp. Usually someone else gasps. But now it's me. Gasping. Trying hard to swallow the truth. "You died a lemon death just like Juliet?" I ask.

"Ask Juliet," she tells me.

"Juliet is here?"

A fire erupts in the old stone hearth. "Yes, I am."

"The two of you died the same lemon death?" I ask.

The flames are swirling upward. "Yes, we did. Many years apart. But we both died a lemon death."

"Get! Out!" I cry.

The fire collapses; the table stops quaking.

Silence.

"I didn't mean it like that, ladies."

The fire erupts once again; the table shakes and spins.

"Thank you," I tell them.

"But Juliet," Chaka says, "why would Derderva want *you* dead? You two didn't even know each other."

“But we did,” our housekeeper of long ago begins, “Derderva and I were no different than Graydove and you.”

“No different than Graydove and me?”

“That’s right. Derderva was my brother.”

“No!” I say.

“Yes!” she insists. “He was much younger than me. He was only eighteen when he killed me. One day I caught him dressing up like Diana Ross and the Supremes, all three of them, and he just lost his mind. I promised that I wouldn’t tell. I told him I would not judge him. I even promised to hem his gowns. But he was not to be reasoned with. He needed me dead so no one would ever find out. And so he killed me.”

“But no,” I correct her. “Nobody killed you, Juliet. You were working for us at the time. You had a stroke.”

We hear classical music playing. Its cadence rises and falls as if it is orchestrating the rising and falling of the flickering light around the room. “I had a stroke,” she tells us. “But it was a stroke brought on by a lemon death.”

I eye my sister. She eyes me back. We scrunch up our foreheads. Neither of us wants to ask. Chaka stares me down, with a roll of the head, as only a black woman can. I relent. “Okay, ladies. Can someone tell us what the heck is a lemon death?”

The spirits laugh. Their laughter is dulcet as birdsong. “A lemon death,” Brenda says, “is a death by lemons. Lemonade spiked with arsenic. I may have suffered a heart attack, but it was a heart attack brought on by poisoning.”

I jump from my chair. I race into the kitchen. I scramble through the cupboards, frantically, desperately searching for the glass pitcher. I am bumped on the head. It hurts. I look up, and there is the pitcher dangling in midair above my head. I leap into the air, trying to grab it. It evades me. I might as well be boxing my own shadow. I cannot make contact. I say “Fuck this” and leave the room. On my entrance into the drawing room, I am bumped on the head again. The pitcher has followed me. I say to it, “Look, down there, you're dripping!" and the pitcher tips to the floor low enough for me to slam it with my fist and send it flying against the wall, where it shatters to the floor. "Faked you out, bastard!" I say triumphantly. I am only now aware of the table of eyes bedazzled by this spectacle of man versus pitcher.

I look at them indignantly. "Derderva tried to poison Chaka and me with his lemonade too! We might have died a lemon death just like Brenda and Juliet. Luckily we forgot to drink it before we went to bed that night, or we never would have woken up."

Chaka rises. "Yes, Gray. You're right."

"So you see, everybody," I say to the group, "Chaka and I are lucky to be alive. Derderva obviously wanted us out of the way. He wanted us dead before we figured out that he killed Father."

"It's too bad that fist of yours destroyed the evidence," Chaka says haughtily.

"No, he didn't destroy the evidence," Plotzman says. I'm surprised to hear the man's voice. He hasn't said much during the séance. I think fear kept him quiet. He may have even gone into shock. But I'm not sure. "We can still analyze the pieces of broken glass," he continues. "But I'm going to need more than that, folks. I mean, I can't exactly reopen this case based on the words of a few...ghosts."

He is drenched now in a waterfall of sweat. His skin is whiter than Mother's summer handbags. "There's no way I can quote ghosts in my police report and take that to the district attorney and say, hey, based on this I think we can get an indictment. I'd get laughed out of the state. I might even get laughed *into* the state...the state hospital!"

A few of us chuckle. Pedro is snoring. Poor baby, darling, boyfriend, Charo. He's tired.

"I don't want to offend anyone, but I need more evidence than this," the detective concludes.

"Go to my house."

It is Brenda.

"Your house?" I ask.

"Yes, the detective should go to my house. To the place where I died. Go to my house and find your evidence. It's all there waiting for you."

"Oh, man," Plotzman says, "this has to be a dream."

"Pedro, pinch him," I suggest.

"Not necessary!" the detective retorts.

Pedro resumes snoring.

"Then go!" Brenda bellows.

"I'll need a warrant."

"Then get a warrant, for chrissake," Brenda wails. "I'm with you in spirit, Plotzman. But you're not making this easy."

"What am I looking for?" he asks.

"Must I tell you everything?"

"Yes, Brenda, you must."

The foundation of the house begins to shift. The whole structure starts to quake. Seismic energy rolls and expands underneath our feet. Oh, boy. Our hands are holding one another so tightly our fingers are carpal-tunneled.

"Go and you will find lemon and arsenic and wire cutters," Brenda says.

"Wire cutters?" Plotzman asks.

"Yes, wire cutters. How else do you think that scoundrel sabotaged *Luftpussy*?"

"*Luftpussy*?" Stevie cries.

"Go!" Brenda roars. "Derderva tried to kill all of you. Go!"

The house has stopped moving and has settled into its original place. We all sigh a deep, exhaustive, heart-pounding collective sigh. Except Detective Plotzman, who is lying on the floor, passed out cold.

Thirty

How to revive a semiconscious police detective?

The prospects puzzle us, one and all.

The spirits are laughing. Truly. Gay laughter swings from the ceilings and flutters from the fireplace.

"Brenda?" I call.

A door slams and the fire goes out, and I think we mortals are left to ourselves and our own devices.

The problem is, we have no devices. That is, until Chaka dashes from the room and returns, moments later, with her cargo plane of a pocketbook. She reaches in. Digs for something. Digs, digs, digs. She pulls out a roll of film, a roll of Scotch tape, and a roll (bulkie with seeds). Next emerges a bottle of Jheri Curl, a *National Geographic,* two plastic spoons, one pack of gum (opened), one pack of gum (unopened). Finally she cries, "Yes!" and withdraws a small medicine kit and snaps it open. "I knew I had something."

She removes two small gauze-like pouches and hands them to Stevie. "Here, put them under his nose."

"What is it?" he asks.

"Ammonia inhalant." she replies.

"Just happen to carry it with you?" he inquires suspiciously.

"Pregnant women occasionally faint, you know," she says. "Now just do it, for chrissake."

He does. First try, nothing. But on the second try the detective comes to, scratching his balls as if he is waking up in the privacy of his own home. Hand madly at work on his testicles, his eyes meet ours and he stops mid ritual, embarrassed, indeed, by the onlookers. He winces. Then simply says, "Explain, please."

We do.

He mutters something about a search warrant and staggers to the door.

"All right, everybody," I say. "Off to Brenda's. We *have* to be there when Derderva is arrested."

"Wouldn't miss it for the world," Chaka concurs.

"*Ay, Dios mio,* Gray. I'm so tired," Pedro whines. It is a whine I can understand. Just looking at this mess of a Charo yanks my heart in all sorts of new and crazy directions.

"I'll put you to bed, my love," I tell him. "Go along without me," I tell the others. "I'll meet you at Brenda's."

☽

The others are gone. Pedro and I are alone. Upstairs in the *Portrait of a Circumcision* bedroom. I have tucked him in. And I'm leaning over him, an arm on either side of his blanketed torso. "You know I love you, Pedro."

He smiles a sleepy grin. "I know."

"But you can go your own way, if you must." A solitary tear rolls down my face. It inches very slowly, pools at my chin, and then drips delicately onto Pedro's lower lip. He washes his tongue over the tear and kisses the air between us. This stirs me and turns my skin to gooseflesh. "I sure hate to lose you," I tell him.

He smiles again. A satisfied grin of clarity. "You're not, Graydove. *Basta,* baby. Enough said."

☽

The place is so quiet now. Pedro fast asleep upstairs. The séance over. The house seems so empty of doubt and confusion, malice and darkness. I blow out candles and put on a few dim lights. I study the photographs hanging on the wall of Father's study (I am in here because I remember seeing an old pair of his hiking boots in one of the closets, which I could use, since it has started raining in furious buckets and without a car I'll need to trek to Brenda's on foot), and I see the whole evolution of our family. Moments of beauty have been captured. Generations have been framed. And so it follows that some of the photographs predate me. They are black-and-white and richer than color. They are history and they are premonitory of the future. Very simply, the evolution continues. Chaka and Kamal will marry. She will have her baby and, hopefully, stop vomiting. From the looks of it, Skye and Stevie will probably marry and have children of their own. And me? Who knows. I'd like to be married someday. Maybe even raise a family. Whatever happens, we are sure to pose for pictures. Photographs will hang.

I pull open the closet and see the boots immediately. I slip them on and head back toward the front door of the house. Discouraged by the rain, I call a cab. And wait.

I hear tires splashing through puddles.

(That was fast.)

I see headlights coming down the driveway. Can't make out much else, the rain is falling so hard in slanted sheets.

A knock on the door.

I swing the door open, saying, "You didn't have to come to the d—" when I realize it is not a cab driver to whom I'm speaking. It is Derderva. His eyeballs are exploding from their sockets; his maniacal mouth is contorted in a way that reminds me of all the times Mother would tell us not to make funny faces lest they freeze that way for the rest of our lives. She spoke with great authority.

"I don't suppose you're here to give me a ride?" I ask.

He says nothing.

"Derderva?"

Nothing.

I want to say "Mona Kahona?" but I fear that might push

him over the edge to which he is clinging. Instead I offer him something to drink. "Lemonade, perhaps?"

He smiles wide and evil. "Lemonade would be lovely, Graydove. Shall I make it?"

"No, Derderva. You're my guest. I'd be happy to make it. I hear my recipe is less toxic than yours."

He grabs me by the arm and squeezes hard. "Look, you filthy-rich spoiled brat. It was only a matter of time before you found me out." He withdraws a handgun from his coat pocket and points it at my chest.

"Found you out?" I ask. "Really, Derderva, I hardly think insulting your lemonade warrants homicide."

He waves the gun. His wrist movements are unsure. So is his face. "What are you saying?"

"I'm saying that it's no big deal if you don't make the best pitcher of lemonade. I'm sure you have other talents," I assure him. "Besides, it's too cold and nasty tonight for lemonade, so why don't you just head on home and we'll forget all about this."

"So I don't have to kill you, Gray?"

"Only if there's some kind of bounty on my head." I laugh a theatrical laugh. Meanwhile my crotch is sweating like a bucket of August in the Mississippi Delta.

He pivots quickly to the door and escapes.

I hear the Yugo making its final whine out of our driveway.

I was not as calm as I sounded. Not even close. My heart was pounding so hard (still is), my hands were clammy and moist, I even think my eyes were fogging up like a windshield on a winter's drive. My intestines are pretzeled up and my bowels feel put upon.

I sit down. Take a deep breath.

The real cab arrives.

I throw on a jacket this time and step toward the door.

"Where are you going, Gray?"

My hands go numb. I sense Derderva has snuck back

into the house and is standing behind me now, the gun to my back.

I turn slowly, very slowly, a gradual, almost unnoticeable pivot. My hands are above my head. Until I realize there's no one there.

"Gray, it's me."

Father.

"Father!"

"Graydove."

I feel embraced. Really, I do. Like a warm breeze has enveloped me, and I look to the ceiling and there he is. More than a voice. More than the presence of the other spirits. I can actually see his face. His hearty, happy, face, the thick white hair atop his head.

"My God!"

"Do you think I would make you do all this work and not thank you?"

"I don't know. So many times we asked to speak with you."

"I know, son. I know. But I wanted to spend a moment with you alone. I will speak to the others later. I want you to know how proud I am of you."

I sit. Overcome, overwhelmed by this tremendous testament to faith. Utterly done in by the power of the other side.

His face is gone now. But his presence remains. Like a splotch of ink in the air.

"The boots look good on you, Gray."

I smile. "Thanks."

"Good job with Derderva. He's heading back into the arms of the police now. He'll be mighty surprised when he returns to Brenda's."

"So, let me guess, Father…you died a lemon death too?"

"No," he replies. "Blunt trauma, just as the autopsy showed. Hit in the head with a rock."

"Oh."

"Derderva tried the lemonade on me. But honestly, I never

drank the stuff. Too tart. I hate tart. He never knew I hated tart. But I did."

"I see."

"Jeez, I am so proud of you, Gray."

"You've said that."

"But I am just beaming. I am the brightest star in heaven tonight."

"Yes, Father, you are one bright star, all right."

"And I am shining down on your mother tonight. She will be so grateful to you, Gray. I know she never lost her faith. Just wait until she hears about all of this."

"All of this?"

There is a deadly silence (appropriate, I suppose). "About tonight, Gray. Our meeting."

"Why, Father?" I ask. "Why the drag shows?"

"Son, I don't expect you to understand."

"I want to."

"I had to be a powerful woman. A woman people cheered."

"Father, please. That's nonsense."

"No, Graydove," he tells me. "It's not. I lived in your mother's shadow for far too long."

"Mother's shadow?"

"The Fortune 500 Celeste Garrison Hoffenstein. She carried the family's business on her own, Gray. She didn't need me. I was a nonperson beside her. She was Margaret Thatcher and I was....hmm...Mr. Thatcher. You see, Mr. Thatcher is so invisible no one even knows his name."

"You needed visibility? Didn't we give you enough attention at home?"

He laughs. "Of course you did. But I could never get the worldwide applause that was bestowed upon your mother. I guess you could say this was my way of acting out. Evening the score."

"But there's no score in a marriage, Father."

"If I had only had the wisdom, the faith, the esteem to know that then," he says softly. "Besides, it was fun. Would you like to hear a number? 'I Will Survive,' perhaps?"

"Gloria Gaynor?"

"My anthem."

He sings. "At first I was afraid...I was petrified..."

"Really, Father, that's unnecessary."

"Thinking I could never live without you as my bride..."

"No, really, Father...I've heard the song."

He tosses out a laugh and it fills the room. Then there is stillness next to the laughter.

"Ah, Gray, had you been ready to see me there, I think you would have enjoyed me onstage at Damsels."

My head is in my hands. I look up. "Maybe so, but come on, Father, Bionica Pie? What the hell was that?"

He snickers. "It was your idea, Gray."

"*My* idea?"

"Sure enough, son. Don't you remember your fascination with the Bionic Woman?"

"Well, yes," I reply.

"Remember how you once asked me if her vagina was bionic too?"

"I just assumed it was, Father."

"And if so, wouldn't her orgasms knock California off the Richter scale?"

"I was somewhat precocious."

"Oh, no, Gray. You were just very much in touch with the Earth... It's something that comes from the Lightfoot side of the family."

"Okay," I say hesitantly. "But what about the *Pie*?"

"The Earth as pie," he explains seamlessly. There is fatherly assumption in his voice. "And pie as vagina."

"Pie as vagina?"

"The Earth moves, my son. The Earth is always moving for someone. I can see it from above," he assures me. "There's a lovely mix of Lightfoot and Hoffenstein in everything, Graydove. Don't you see?"

"Gee, Father. How do I explain this to everyone?"

"However you wish," he replies. "I only hope you won't be ashamed of me."

I begin to cry, remembering words not unlike those when, years ago, I came out to my parents and I was worried and scared and confused and they both just hugged me and thanked me and told me to get a haircut if I ever wanted to find a boyfriend. I told them how frightened I was that they would be ashamed of me. And then my father pulled me close and said, "We could never be ashamed of you, Graydove. Never. We love you. There is no shame in a family that has love."

I weep throughout this entire memory, unaware of how long or short it lingers. I feel a hand against my cheek now, but see nothing but air. I allow the wispy touch to penetrate my skin, and out loud I say, "Thank you, Father, for being my father."

Oh Dad, Poor Dad, You Went Into Mother's Closet and Came Out in Drag (Or, Some Thoughts on This Whole Matter One Year Later)

Mother got out of jail just in time for Christmas and Hanukkah, and, now with Kamal Kareem in the family, Kwanzaa. She's a different lady. Prison has changed her in ways we least expected. She can now cook. She wears less cashmere and much more linen. She is still very elegant but less apt to Concorde off to Paris at the drop of a beret. She is a more serious woman; she reads more, talks less. She still schedules herself for manicures and pedicures, but the cosmetics on her face mask less age and reveal more truth, more character; the pancake has thinned, the shadows around her eyes have darkened.

Mother decided she was tired of selling parking meters around the globe, so she sold Parking Meters of the World for three hundred and fifty-seven million dollars to the homophobic morons who had me fired, and she has used some of the money to open up transitional homes for women who need a place to stay when they get out of jail. Like a halfway house but more luxurious. More like a spa for former criminals. "They each deserve at least a taste of the life I've been fortunate to live," Mother said at one of the ribbon cuttings, unashamed of the country club ambience. "The women," she reminds everyone, "must complete an academic program and go through counseling." The very best go on to college and graduate school, where Mother hopes they will earn MBAs, financed through a generous foundation she has set up for the next three hundred and forty-five years (the number of days she was incarcerated).

Mother insisted on naming her halfway homes (there are plans to build one in every state) "CeCe's House." We hate the name, but you don't tell a woman who, instead of jetting between Palm Beach, the Riviera, and Martha's Vineyard, spent a year in jail for a crime she didn't commit, what to do.

Derderva committed the crime that Mother did not.

That was decided by a jury about ten months after his arrest that stormy night in early December. He was actually convicted on first-degree murder charges for the four separate murders of Juliet, Brenda, Stevie's mechanic, and Father. Bodies (or remains thereof) were exhumed, evidence collected. The remains were reburied with little fanfare. "Oh, just dump what's left of me in a garden somewhere," Brenda told us after the prosecutors had sampled what they needed. "And let us nourish the flowers." Juliet agreed. So did Father. It's been very hard to convince the authorities that we've been communicating with the dead. Thank God, they managed to gather good evidence without sitting around that small table in the drawing room of *Entre Tetas*.

I go there often, still. And talk to Father. He regrets blurting out the truth to Mother that night. It was done in a fit of anger and frustration. He should have found a more delicate, sensitive way to tell her he had been stealing her gowns. But that is indeed what they were fighting about the night of his death. She had been asking why no parking meters had been sold to Russia. Having never actually gone to Russia, Father had no answer. She grilled him. "How can you go to Russia once a month for five years and come home empty-handed?" she asked. "For God's sake, Colin, the damn Russians just woke up from a coma of Communism. They're ready to *consume*! They're ready to *buy*! Anything and everything from the West!"

Father said nothing.

"You make me think I can't trust you with a travel budget!" Mother persisted. "I'm talking to you like a boss, not like a wife, Colin. You've brought in no business to speak of. The board wants me to fire you. What should I tell them you've been doing all this time?"

"Drag."

And so the truth came out. A long explanation, punctuated by screaming and yelling, vocal spasms that buckled the windows. Then the wine glass was tossed. To spite his wife of many years, Colin Lightfoot Hoffenstein quickly shed the wine-stained shirt and made off for Mother's dressing room. He borrowed one of her finest gowns, threw on a wig, and reappeared in the dining room, where Mother burst into tears as she followed him to the front door and slammed it behind him. (Mother has still not come to terms with Father's secret life. We try to talk about it, but she refuses, insisting Father stormed out of the house in drag that night just to shock her, or maybe embarrass her. "He probably knocked on every door in Chilmark just to say hello and humiliate me." She doesn't even believe there is a Damsels. We've offered to take her there. She refuses.)

But as Father tells it, he was not knocking on any doors in Chilmark. He was taking a long walk, crossing that infamous bridge on Chappaquiddick, when he saw a figure approach from the opposite side. A woman, her hair in a bonnet. It was night;he could only make out her dark curves as she moved toward him. And then, under a gauzy light cast from a pole at mid bridge, he recognized the face: Mona Kahona.

"Mona?"

"Yes?"

"It's me, Bionica...Pie."

"Bionica Pie! What are you doing on my island? I told you I never want to set eyes on you again!"

"You told me never to step foot in Damsels again, darling Mona, but don't for one minute think you can tell me which bridge I can cross."

"I really should have done away with you the other night."

"With everyone watching us in the alley? Too many witnesses."

"Well, there aren't too many here."

That's when Father sustained the first blow to his head. Mona's fist swiped him hard, hard enough that he fell to his knees, and then Mona launched a foot into his face. Father then remembers being dragged ("Yes, Gray, that's a lovely pun, *dragged*") to the other side of the bridge and rolled down an embankment to the water. Mona then lifted a rock from the shoreline and slammed it into Father's already shaken skull.

And he was dead.

But his eyes were open.

Wide open.

The dead man saw what Mona did next.

Mona pulled off Father's gown and the wig, expressed little surprise or regret that the deceased Bionica Pie was none other than Colin Lightfoot Hoffenstein ("Now no one will suspect it was drag queen versus drag queen," she whispered to his corpse), and left Father not to a lemon death, but to a death completely free of citrus.

I related this story to Pedro not long after I heard it from Father, and he listened, eyes agape, and then clutched on to me for the rest of the night as we slept under piles of blankets and quilts. We were at *Entre Tetas* for what I assumed was one last weekend together, one final farewell to the man-man love pair we had been. I had held my tears all weekend. I had looked the other way, away from the shining brilliance of his face and the glare it caused my vulnerable eyes.

And so in bed that night, holding me fiercely, fearfully,

Pedro said, "Gray, I need to tell you something." His voice was shaking. There was even vibrato in his breath as it hit the skin of my neck.

"Yes?"

He lifted his head up from the slope of my neck and fixed his eyes on mine so desperately; I sensed a need in him to absorb every molecule of who I am. "I'm not going through with it," he said. "I'm not having the sex change."

I shook my head, confused a bit. Dazed and surprised. "No?"

"No."

"Why not?"

He took a deep breath. "After seeing what being a woman did to your father, I think it's too risky."

I ran my hand across his brow. "Baby, I didn't tell you Father's story to scare you."

"I know," he said. "But it wasn't just the story you told me tonight. It's the whole thing. I was at the séance that night. I heard all the ghosts..."

"Spirits..."

"Whatever...I heard them. I saw what happened. And I don't ever plan to sit around that table again. It freaks me out just being back here in this house."

"I understand, Pedro. Really, I do," I told him. "But how do I know you won't change your mind? About the sex change?"

"If there were ever a message from up above, that was it," he said. "It was like a warning or something, Gray. I don't know, but what happened to your father is not going to happen to me."

"But Father didn't have a sex change," I reminded him.

"Are you trying to talk me out of staying with you just the way I am?"

And then the tears came. They came so fast there was no chance to steel myself. My skin started tingling, and I just lay there and sobbed. He held me tight, and I felt this strange sensation of butter melting on my chest. I realized, of course, what all of this meant. Pedro would not become a woman, and Pedro would stay with me. I would not lose him. He would be my man, and I his. We celebrated without announcing we were celebrating. We held each other so tight and made love loudly enough to scare the spirits away.

Of course this new development made it necessary for me (rather happily and without a shred of misgiving) to see my boss, Ben, and tell him that our first kiss was our last kiss and that, romantically, we had no future together.

"Romance?" he asked coarsely. "Who was talking romance, Gray? I just wanted to suck your dick dry and fuck your hungry asshole."

"How pornographic of you," I replied, then paused, and then I sliced at his memory with "You said you loved me."

"Men will say anything to get dick."

How true.

I quit my job.

I was in no hurry to find another. It wasn't like I couldn't keep busy. I had a wedding to plan. I proposed and Pedro accepted and we both bought each other engagement rings that make the Hope Diamond look, well, hopeless.

It's hard enough to plan one wedding. Imagine planning three.

It was a triple wedding, actually. Chaka and Kamal Kareem stated their vows, followed by Stevie and Skye, followed by Pedro and me. The event was held in an abandoned Eastern Airlines hangar at Logan Airport. It was the only place large enough to hold the thousands of people invited. It was also very convenient for the considerable number of guests (including a duke, a duchess, a mistress, and that Greek heiress with the bladder control problem) who had to fly in from foreign places to attend. Beautiful, really. Mother cried the most during my vows with Pedro. "I never thought I'd live to see this day," she told me later. "I worried most about you. About you being a sad, lonely homosexual. It does my heart good to know you have a man to take care of you."

No use explaining to Mother that I didn't need a man to take care of me any more than she ever had. All I could say to her was, "Most homosexuals are not lucky enough to have a family like this, Mother."

She burst into tears all over again.

For wedding gifts, Mother bought Chaka and Kamal Kareem a house, Stevie and Skye a plane, and Pedro and me oceanfront property in Puerto Rico, where she thinks he and I can build a beautiful guesthouse someday and have a little business for ourselves.

"No hurry," she assured us.

So, with an abundance of time on my hands, I decided to visit my brother, Kirkland, on the West Coast. "Visit" might not be exactly the right word; "confront" is perhaps more appropriate. I wanted to know why he never showed up at the wedding. I wanted to know why he has not expressed any interest in the family, particularly in Mother, who hadn't heard from him since her celebrated release from state prison. He offered little explanation and no apology. He did want to know, however, if I had flown out there first-class. When I said, "No, I didn't," he looked at me puzzled and shrugged his mean shoulders. "You will someday, Gray," he told me. "With the money I've inherited from Father, and the money we're all getting from the sale of the company, I plan to buy myself an airline. I'm not sure which one, Gray. What do you think? Delta? Northwest? United?"

"I don't know," I replied. "But if anyone can wage a hostile takeover, Kirkland, you can."

Truth is, I don't need Kirkland's airline. And I never will. Stevie's new plane is big enough to seat fifty. Stevie does not call the new plane *Luftpussy II*. Marriage has matured him; besides, I told him I would never fly with him again if he used that name. Instead, he calls the plane *Cloudholder*, and I am very happy about that.

Now that the wedding is over and done with, I've started teaching accounting courses three nights a week at Northeastern University. In my off time, I'm taking flying lessons. Flying is changing my life.

Sometimes Stevie serves as my instructor. He's very patient and forgiving (even when I roll or loop the plane by mistake). We fly sometimes over Martha's Vineyard, over Brenda's house, over *Entre Tetas,* and exchange knowing smiles. Occasionally, Chaka flies with me too. She still throws up a lot, even though she's no longer pregnant (the baby, Colynn Daisy Softmeadow Lashondra Hoffenstein Moorehead, is doing fine). And, of course, Pedro takes to the sky with me every now and then (the flutter of the plane usually rocks him into a gentle sleep). I love flying with him in the golden hours of a late summer afternoon. The earth below glimmers and shimmers like a precious stone. The velvet sky around us is soaked in roselight. This is where I'll talk to Father sometimes. This is where I'll ask after Brenda and everyone else. And then I'll look to the man I love, seated beside me, his seat belt low and tight around his waist, and watch as he closes his eyes softly and becomes, like an angel, a part of my heaven.

About the Author

Steven Cooper is an Emmy award-winning television news anchor and reporter. Born and raised in Massachusetts, he also calls Phoenix and Orlando home. *With You in Spirit* is his first novel.